The Green Kingdom

An Eco-fable

Eric Chaline

Eric Chaline Books, Islington, London

© Eric Chaline, 2021, 2022

All rights reserved. No part of this publication may be reproduced, stored in a retrieval system, or transmitted in any form or by any means (including electronic, mechanical, photocopying, recording, or otherwise) without prior written permission from the author.

ISBN- 9798790745201

For information about custom editions, special sales, and premium and corporate purchases, please contact the author or Kindle Direct Publishing.

Printed on demand by Kindle Direct Publishing

Design and illustrations by Eric Chaline and Kindle Direct Publishing

Conceived, designed, and produced by
Eric Chaline and Kindle Direct Publishing.

Prologue

Visions

A lone warrior, armour-clad and helmeted, stands on the battlements of the highest tower of the Citadel. As the observer's eye swoops down towards the lonely figure, she removes the high-crested helmet and sets it aside on the parapet. A single tress of hair that was tucked inside the helmet slowly uncoils down her back like a snake.

"Chirrip!"

"Where have you been?" she scolds the small creature that skips towards her along the parapet. It could be some kind of lemur or an exotic species of squirrel, with a long prehensile tail and golden fur striped with dark-green streaks.

"Chirrip!" it replies.

She smiles and holds out her hand. It jumps easily onto her outstretched palm and climbs up her arm to her shoulder.

From her vantage point, the Green Kingdom unfolds like a tapestry of fortresses, encampments, villages, towns and cities. The yellow sun hangs high in a cloudless blue sky. She shades her green-on-green eyes, with their irises flecked with gold, and watches, as ant-like, the tribes of the kingdom migrate, build, trade, gather and fight, as they have always done, as they will always do. In the apparent chaos, there is a hidden order and pattern that she can discern. But there is something else; something she cannot quite identify: a discordance that makes her feel suddenly ill at ease. She scans the plain again, seeking out the cause of her anxiety, like an orchestral conductor looking for the one musician in who has played a false note.

She blinks and, in an instant, the familiar scene is transformed. The blue sky is black and starless; columns of red flame and smoke scorch the plain; cries of pain, terror and anguish rise up towards her.

Horror-struck, she has to steady herself on the parapet. Chirrip screeches in fear and buries his head in her hair. A glow directly above makes her look up. A fireball bursts out of the clouds with a sound louder than a thunderclap. It passes the tower three arm's lengths away from her – so close that she can feel its scorching heat on her face. She leans over the parapet to follow its path. It gouges through the wooden walkways below, sending up a huge fountain of fire and flaming debris. Two of the neighbouring towers explode into flame. Men, women, children and animals are running in panic along the walkways, showered by burning debris. There's no escape from the flames and the collapsing buildings. More fireballs scorch fiery trails through the clouds, smashing into the towers, walkways and walls of the Citadel. The base of the tower on which she stands is burning. The flames that devour the tower's outer walls, race upwards towards her.

"This can't be real!" she screams, half in disbelief and half in terror.

She blinks. The horrible vision is gone as quickly as it had come. The sun shines over the undulating plain and the intricately choreographed movements of its inhabitants. She looks down at the Citadel below. The walkways, walls and towers are intact; the inhabitants go about their daily business.

She wonders if she's going mad, but she has little time to think. She blinks again. The sky is no longer blue but a cauldron of roiling grey-black clouds that hang low over the plain, spewing bolts of lightning that earth themselves every few seconds. A distant roaring sound makes her look over across the plain. A grey-green wall flecked with white fills the horizon in every direction like a new circuit of mountains. But mountains do not move. In one horrified moment, she realises that it's a gigantic wall of water almost as high as the tower she stands on. It sweeps towards the Citadel, pulverizing everything in its path – no house, encampment or fortress can resist the tsunami's destructive power. It smashes into the outer walls of the city. They resist for a few seconds before they, too, are breached; water floods into the Citadel, sweeping away men, women, children and animals. The towers sway wildly and topple, crashing into one another.

She blinks again. The roar of the waters is silenced, and the world is suddenly still again. The water that flowed through the streets has turned into ice. She's never felt such cold, her limbs freeze, her blood congealing in her veins.

She blinks again. The world is as it was once more. The air is calm and warm, and the Citadel and plain beyond are whole. She braces herself for a new vision of horror and destruction. The air in front of her begins to shimmer. Swirling shapes without colour or substance twist and distort the fabric of the air like a heat haze on a hot summer's day. This, at least, is a familiar sight: an Unseen One has crossed the barrier between the kingdoms and manifests itself in front of her.

"Hail, Eireis, Caller of the Argaë," the Unseen One says, its voice faint, as if it were coming from a great distance.

Eireis is puzzled. "Why are you here? I have not summoned you. Look at the sun, we are still many days away from the Calling." But, at that moment, she realises that she has no idea what time it is, or how she came to be standing on the battlements of the Archon's Tower high above the Citadel.

"Do not be troubled, Caller," the Unseen One says. "I come to you with a message from the Soul of the World. The things you have seen are dream-visions of what has happened in ages past and may again in ages yet to come, while your body is safe in the sleep of Whiteday."

"Dream-visions?" she asks uncertainly.

"A time of trial is to come – destruction and death for the Argaë and many of the tribes of the Green Kingdom. Although things have been done that cannot be undone, not everything that you have seen may yet come to pass. There is still time to choose; there is always a choice."

"What do you mean we must choose?" she asks confused. "We have ever followed the ways of the Argaë lore, every Greenday and Whiteday from the beginnings of the Green Kingdom."

"But soon, you and the other tribes of the Green Kingdom must choose," the Unseen One says. "The Soul of the World bids me tell you that one will come who will cross the bridge between the kingdoms. At first, he will appear weak and helpless, and you must help him. He is your hope for the future. You will know him by his sky-tinted eyes...." The Unseen One's voice fades to a sigh. "Remember … you will know him by his sky-tinted eyes...."

"Come back! I don't understand!" Eireis calls out. But she feels the world slipping away from her. The tower, the Citadel and the plain beyond become insubstantial and fade into darkness as Eireis falls back into the sleep of Whiteday.

* * *

Now look down on a quite different scene: in a suburban bedroom, on a cold, rainy afternoon, Daniel sat at his desk with its view of the garden, streaming a movie on his tablet. An only child, he'd watched many movies to pass the time during successive lockdowns. He preferred fantasy movies in which the protagonists began weak and pathetic: the likes of Harry Potter, Frodo, Lira, or Alice. But as if by magic, Daniel thought bitterly, more often than not, with a great deal of magic at their disposal, in the shape of wands and invisibility cloaks, rings of power, golden compasses and potions, they became brave and resourceful. After that, it was easy for them. They had an easily identified enemy, and all they had to do was to defeat them to make everything right. But Daniel knew the real world wasn't like that. There was no magic, and there were no Voldemort, no Dark Lord, no Snow Queen, no Mrs Coulter to overcome to save the world. Real life was a lot more complicated, and no amount of wishing would make it easier to deal with.

He'd seen this instalment of the Harry Potter franchise so many times that he wasn't really paying attention, so it took him a few moments to notice that something wasn't quite right with the film. The dialogue and background music had stopped. He thought the film must be buffering, but when he looked at the tablet, Harry, Ron and Hermione were straight back at him out of the screen. He was so surprised that he almost turned around to see if they were looking at someone standing behind him.

"Are you going to sit there watching movies all day long?" Harry asked in a tone of voice that Daniel didn't like at all.

Daniel was surprised, but also struck by the thought that if he and other people like him didn't watch the movies over and over, there would be no Harry Potter, and Daniel Radcliffe would be just another actor you barely noticed on TV.

He was about to say something when Hermione said portentously, "I bring a message from the Soul of the World. A time of trial is coming," she said. "Look outside."

Daniel looked up, and saw the garden engulfed a blazing inferno; the trees on the far side of the rear wall, black skeletal outlines within the flames; he blinked, and the fire was gone, replaced by murky, brownish-green water that filled the garden and lapped against his windowsill; he blinked again, and the water had frozen solid. Another blink the garden was back to the way it had been a few moments earlier: muddy, the green of the grass muted under the slate-grey sky.

"Although things have been done that cannot be undone," Harry said. "Not everything that has been predicted may yet come to pass. There's still time to choose; there's always a choice."

Daniel was about to ask Harry what he meant about choosing, when he realised that he must be dreaming. "This is a dream, isn't it?" he said.

"Of course, you're dreaming," Ron cut in. "What difference does that make?"

Hermione hushed him and said, "The Soul of the World bids me tell you that one will come to you; one who can cross the bridge between the worlds. At first, she'll appear strong and confident, but she will need your help. She is your hope for the future. You will know her by her green-on-green eyes...." Hermione's voice faded to a sigh. "Remember ... you will know her by his green-on-green eyes...."

"Come back! I don't understand!" Daniel called out. But the movie has resumed and the characters have moved on.

– 1 –

A Rainy Sunday

Daniel could hear his parents' raised voices, insistent though muted by the closed bedroom door. He tried to concentrate on the film on his tablet. He was watching the first Harry Potter movie, because in *The Philosopher's Stone*, Harry, Ron and Hermione were closest to him in age. They were eleven, and he was almost eleven – well, he'd had his tenth birthday a couple of months back, but he figured that it was only a matter of time until he would be eleven.

When the action in the movie slowed and the soundtrack grew quieter, it couldn't drown out the counterpoint of his father's tenor to his mother's alto. The argument had been brewing since morning. Sometimes, when they argued, he kept score; sometimes, he escaped into the fantasy that he wasn't really their son but an orphan – a very special orphan, of course – living with resentful relatives – but who'd soon be rescued by a magical stranger. But often, like today, their constant sparring made him feel anxious and depressed.

Daniel's parents worried about their only son, but the way they expressed their concern tended to make things worse. His father tried to encourage him but didn't have any patience with him if he failed to show any enthusiasm and aptitude for whatever he thought should interest him. As for his mother, he'd once overheard her on the phone telling a friend that she was worried about his socialisation, because he'd had so much time off school during the pandemic. He thought that if he did have a poor socialisation – whatever it was – it was probably because he had parents who found it so difficult to get along. Maybe socialisation was like Harry's psychic link to Voldemort.

At least, the lockdowns, which had forced the family to stay cooped up at home, were over, but it was that time of year when the weatherman encouragingly announces the end of winter, but spring is yet to make itself felt. They'd had a few days of sunshine that week – not warm, but mild enough for a drive out of town where he could fly the drone his father had bought him for his birthday – though he suspected that his dad would be doing most of the flying, at least, until he got bored of it, before letting him have a go. If his parents were in a good mood, they'd go to a child-friendly pub or restaurant afterwards. But Saturday had dawned overcast and frozen, with sleet and snow forecast to last until the end of Sunday, which meant no outing. Without regards to logic, the adults were blaming one another for the change of plan. All they'd needed to do was to check the forecast the night before.

The skirmishing had begun over breakfast with small things that would have gone unnoticed by a stranger but were all too obvious to Daniel: although his father hadn't finished eating, his mother had begun to clear up.

"I think I'll have another round of toast, if you don't mind, dear," his father said, not looking up from his phone. His father only ever called his mother "dear" when he wanted to annoy her. It was what his own father, Daniel's granddad, Dan senior, had called his wife during fifty years of married life. His mother didn't reply but grudgingly returned the butter dish and jar of marmalade to the table, before ramming two slices of bread into the toaster. Daniel mumbled that he was going to his room and slunk away from the table, but neither parent noticed his departure.

A frozen sleety rain began to fall, ending the slightest hope of diversion. They'd have to stay home all day. His parents had managed to keep apart for most of the morning: his mother, Caroline, driving to the supermarket to get a few things she needed for the Sunday lunch that she hadn't expected to cook; his father, Jeff, busying himself with chores in the house. A little past one, the family had sat down to lunch. His parent had not talked to one another but continued the morning's argument through him; his father quizzed him about his chances of getting picked for the football team, which were slim to zero, though Jeff held on to the hope Daniel might show some athletic aptitude for sport; his mother asked him about homework and teachers.

"What would you say if we built a swimming pool in the garden, Daniel?" Caroline asked brightly. "You'd like that, wouldn't you?"

"Oh! Very environmentally friendly! Very green!" Jeff commented snidely. "How often can you use a pool in this country? Think of our blessed carbon footprint you're always going on about! A tennis court or basketball hoop would be much better. Don't you think, Daniel?" It annoyed her when he called him Daniel.

"We could use rainwater and heat it with solar panels," Caroline said, refusing to give up on the idea.

Jeff rolled his eyes, as a comment on the impracticality of womankind in general and of his wife in particular. They both looked at him, but he stared into his bowl of cereal and said nothing, knowing better than to take sides. If they really wanted to know, which they didn't, he preferred the garden the way it was.

The argument moved onto familiar territory. Caroline was worried about the environment – though usually, Daniel had to admit, her concern increased with distance, so that places like the rainforests of Indonesia and Brazil, and the wildlife of Africa and the Amazon counted far more than their own degraded environment. Jeff, out of mischief, countered that the environment had managed to survive perfectly well for the past few million years, and he saw no reason which it shouldn't carry on doing so. Daniel prayed that they wouldn't get started on climate change, in which his father feigned to disbelieve but solely to get a rise out of his wife.

* * *

Daniel and his parents had moved from their city-centre flat into their new suburban home the January before the first lockdown. They'd been lucky, they'd thought, to have made it out of the city just in time. But they'd quickly changed their minds when Jeff had begun to work from home, and Daniel had been off school as well.

On the day of the move, the adults had been irritable after a week of bickering and packing. The slow, tedious drive to the suburbs behind the lumbering removal van through weekday morning traffic had done little to improve their mood. It was past one o'clock when they'd arrived, and Jeff was doubly annoyed when the movers had announced that they were going to break an hour for lunch. He'd sworn under his breath, and the family, too, had driven to the nearest pub where they'd sat down to a dismal lunch in a soulless family room. It was gone two when the movers had begun to move the family's possessions into the house.

Their new home was much older than the surrounding houses. Fifty or so years earlier, when Jeff's great-grandfather had bought the house and surrounding land, it had been a working farm, called Greenacres, which stood alone in the middle of fields, pastures and copses – the remains of a much larger native forest that had been eaten away by the creeping tide of development that was soon to leave the farm a stranded relic of a defunct way of life. It was a beached oddity among the detached, suburban homes built for city professionals during the eighties and nineties.

The house stood at the end of a short unpaved cul-de-sac off the paved road and was as unlike its neighbours as it could contrive to be. Where they had freshly painted render or hardwood or metal cladding, the farm's weathered bricks were exposed, pitted and scarred by the years; its lichen-encrusted roof was tiled rather than slated. But what really set it apart was its large walled garden, which backed onto a small stand of trees, which was one the area's few remaining open spaces other than the local park and golf course.

Daniel had been excited and eager to help with the move, but whenever he'd picked up a carton or chair and asked his mother where she wanted it, she'd get annoyed and exclaim, "Oh, put that down, Daniel! I don't know where it'll go yet!"

Jeff, who'd insisted on supervising the unloading of the larger pieces of furniture, had been no more encouraging. "Can't you see we're busy, Daniel," he'd said with his hands firmly in his pockets as two removal men struggled with a sofa. "Be careful with that!" he'd said upbraiding the movers. "It's brand new."

His offers of help rejected, Daniel had retreated to the kitchen and peered into the garden through the grimy panes of glass of the back door. Whereas the other houses had compact gardens that the owners contrived to make even smaller by installing decking, slate patios and paved outdoor rooms, the farm's half-acre garden looked spacious and child friendly. Unfortunately, nothing had been done in the last few months, when Dan senior had left for what had turned out to be an extended stay in hospital, followed by convalescence in a nursing home.

Dan senior had never had a day's illness in his life, until his seventy-fifth birthday when he'd had a heart attack. Although his heart trouble had been successfully treated, it had been triggered a stroke that had left him partially paralyzed on the right side. The hospital had told his son and daughter-in-law that he wouldn't be able to look after himself. After several heated discussions that differed from their usual rows because they didn't concern themselves with their relationship or Daniel, Jeff and Caroline had agreed to move the family from their inner-city flat to Greenacres to look after Dan senior when he was well enough to leave the nursing home. Neither Jeff nor Caroline relished the idea of living with Dan senior, with whom relations were strained at best, but the alternative – paying for residential care – was out of the question. Only Daniel had been pleased. Although his grandfather was often distant and cold, not really knowing how to deal with his grandson, Daniel quite liked him. He didn't nag him like his mother, nor get exasperated with him like his father.

An overgrown flagstone path led from the back door across a lawn studded with saplings and fungi and patched with encroaching nettles and thistles. A deckchair stood to one side of the path close to the back door, where Dan senior had left it the last time he'd used it the previous summer, no doubt expecting to sit in it the following day. The varnish was cracked and peeling, and the canvas was stained and rotting after being left out in the rain and snow through autumn and winter.

The lawn was enclosed by flowerbeds, in which leggy rosebushes, their un-pruned canes sprouting in disorder, were visible above the tangle of dead weeds. Beyond the beds at the far end of the lawn was a fence, built to separate the ornamental beds and lawn from the working garden behind it, with access provided by an ornamental arch, now, like the fence, smothered in ivy. The rear garden consisted of a vegetable plot, a cage for soft fruit, from which Daniel was allowed to pick fat raspberries and juicy currants in the summer, a greenhouse, a shed, a pond, and most mysterious and attractive of all in a scary way, a beehive, which his mother never tired of telling him was strictly off-limits.

He wondered what had become of the bees without Dan senior. Had they upped and flown away? Swarmed, his grandfather had once explained – when a queen led part of the colony away, or sometimes, when there was something wrong with the hive: a sickness that made the bees abandon it altogether. Once, when his parents had dropped him off at his grandparents to attend a child-free wedding, Dan senior had kitted him out in his own beekeeper's hat and veil that were so big for him that he felt he was wearing a tent and led him to within a few feet of the forbidden hive, with strict orders not to move. He'd stood there frozen, not daring to breathe. Dan senior had begun by inspecting the hive's exterior for any cracks or holes where a predator might enter unobserved.

"They'll fight to the death to defend the entrance," Dan senior had explained. "But if a wasp manages to come in through a hole, they're defenceless once it's inside." As he worked, he'd chatted to the hive – to the queen within – as if she were an old friend. "They're trying to push through the planning for them new houses over the wall. I'll be sorry to see those trees go if they get the go ahead. Don't seem right," he went on. "I grew up with them trees, known them all my life."

That wasn't all: the developers had made Dan senior an offer for the rear half of the garden, but he'd turned them down flat. When they'd found out about the offer, Jeff and Caroline's reaction had been predictable. Caroline had been outraged and spoken about forming an action committee to oppose the development, while Jeff had suggested that, as the garden was so large and Dan senior wasn't getting any younger, he might as well sell and have a little nest egg set by in case of an emergency. But the initial planning application had been turned down, and, as far as Daniel knew, the development had been put on hold.

His inspection finished Dan senior had made Daniel move back a little, before he'd lifted off the hive's roof and sprayed smoke inside from a battered metal can shaped like a coffee pot – to calm the bees and make them more docile, he'd explained. A few of the livelier bees had flown up, but most had stayed quiescent, crawling protectively over the comb. Dan senior had placed his hand inside the hive and made a high-pitched trilling whistle and waited. After a few minutes he'd removed his hand. A bee larger than the others sat in the middle of his grandfather's palm. A few attendant bees fussed around her, but the larger bee seemed quite happy.

"This is the queen," his grandfather had said. "Say hello and bow to Her Majesty."

Daniel had bowed clumsily, "Hello, Your Majesty," he'd said, trying not to trip over the unaccustomed words and his own feet.

The queen attended by a squadron of ladies in waiting had taken off from Dan senior's hand and flown towards Daniel. Dan senior had stared in astonishment as the queen and her retinue hovered immediately in front of Daniel, peering at him through the protective veil. The queen had flown to within a few inches of Daniel face. Unconcerned, Daniel had lifted the veil to get a better look.

The thousands of lenses that made up her compound eyes acted like prisms scattering the light so that they changed colour as she hovered, sometimes a glossy brown or lacquer-black, sometimes an iridescent blue that shaded into green and purple. She'd stared into his pale blue eyes the colour of the sky in early summer. Everything had fallen silent around them, apart from the buzz of insect wings, which, for a few seconds, had seemed to resonate with the faintest sounds of voices calling out his name.

"Well, I'll be...." the old man had said amazed, snapping Daniel out of his trance.

The queen had flown back to the hive and disappeared into the roiling mêlée of insect bodies. Dan senior had quickly replaced the roof on the hive. He'd stared at Daniel for a few moments. Bees were strange creatures, after all. There was no question of being able to understand everything they did. "Best if you don't tell your mother," he'd said. "You know what she's like."

* * *

The back door was locked, but a large key labelled "kitchen" lay invitingly on the worktop. It was a large wrought-iron key like the one to Wonderland Alice had found, but here the door was normal-sized. Daniel looked at it longingly for several minutes. His parents were already in a bad mood. They'd get even more annoyed if he unlocked the back door and went into the garden without asking for permission first. His mother would be concerned about his safety, which would irritate his father, who'd sooner or later take it out on him.

He was never able to please both parents at the same time. His mother was always worrying about him, as if he were a porcelain doll that might shatter at the slightest knock. If she ever found him climbing a wall or doing anything she considered remotely hazardous, she'd panic and scream for him to stop. His father was the exact opposite and got annoyed if he showed any timidity or fear, calling him a cry-baby until Daniel ran off in tears. He was still weighing up the risks when his mother came in leading two removal men carrying cartons labelled "kitchen". "These go in here," she told them.

"Mum, can I go into the garden?" Daniel asked hesitantly.

"What?" She looked momentarily suspicious. But when she saw that the garden was enclosed by a wall too high to climb and was already in such a state of dilapidation that nothing Daniel could do could possibly make it worse, she'd agreed. "Put your old school coat and gloves on… and your wellies, it looks muddy out there and stay on the lawn where I can see you. And don't climb any trees."

"There aren't any trees, mum," he pointed out, but she hadn't noticed as she was now busy deciding where the movers should stack the kitchen cartons. Normally she wouldn't had let him go out on his own, even though he was almost eleven, but she was so distracted that she'd agreed and unlocked the back door for him.

He ran upstairs and put on last year's school coat, which was now too small for him, his wellies and mittens and was back downstairs in seconds.

"Well, if only you were that fast when it's time to go to school, young man," his mother said as she opened the back door. A gust of cold air, laden with the smells of wet earth and rotting leaves, blew into the kitchen.

"Well, go on. What are you waiting for?" She said, shooing him out. She shut the door behind him to keep out the cold from an already chilly house. Jeff, the tech wizard, she'd said sarcastically, had been unable to reset the old-fashioned boiler timer, and it was only when she'd found the right video on Youtube that the problem had been resolved. There were two worn stone steps down to the flagstone path, which were covered with moss and slippery from the morning's melted frost. He almost slipped but managed to keep his balance. He half expected his mother to open the door and call him back in, but her attention had been distracted and she hadn't noticed.

He surveyed his new kingdom. Back in the city, the mansion block was surrounded by a manicured garden in which it was forbidden to play or run. If he ever did, it would earn him a tut-tut from the chairman of the residents committee who seemed to patrol the garden in the afternoon in search of skipping, running or footballing miscreants. Daniel knew that nature shouldn't be like that: tamed and straightjacketed like some ornamental accessory. The garden of Greenacres was now a wilderness. It was the first time he'd seen so many weeds and saplings in what was meant to be a garden.

He followed the path that divided the lawn into two equal halves, stopping to examine the derelict deckchair. The canvas had once been a cheerful blue and yellow stripe, but the colours had faded to shades of dirty grey. Large rosettes of green-black mould pockmarked the material. The chair's feet seemed to have taken root in thick tussocks of grass.

He picked up a branch from the lawn and poked at the rotten canvas, which disintegrated. He looked guiltily around to see if his mother had seen him, but there was no censorious face at the kitchen window. Nevertheless, he flung the stick as far away as he could, stuck his hands in his pockets and tried to look innocent until he was sure it was safe. The beds held little of interest: weeds and saplings crowded around the shrubs, slowly starving them of light, water and nutrients. He promised them he would "liberate" them, when he got his mother's permission and weeding instructions, and squelched back to the path.

He played hopscotch, hopping and sliding on the mossy flagstones, making up all kinds of rules and challenges as he went along: he'd have to go back one hop if he landed on a crack or on the grass. Before he was aware of it, he'd reached the archway leading into the forbidden rear garden, which was now so overgrown that only an opening a few inches wide remained in the ivy.

The mass of dark glossy leaves looked like the surface of a murky pond somehow set vertically across his path. The kind that his parents constantly warned him about, even though, he thought bitterly, he was already a good swimmer (it was the one sport he was good at and genuinely enjoyed). He put his gloved hand through the opening, half expecting something to pull him through from the far side. But the only thing that he'd felt had been the snapping of hundreds of tiny threads. As he pulled his hand back, he saw that his glove was covered in the silvery filaments of spider's web.

Parting the ivy carefully to avoid any creepy crawlies, Daniel poked his head through. Any further advance was prevented by a gigantic briar almost six feet high that occupied the whole width of the back garden. Beyond it, he could see the tops of the stand of trees on the other side of the garden wall, their denuded branches like elongated black fingers against the grey afternoon sky. Somewhere within the brown tangle was the fruit cage, vegetable plot, greenhouse, pond and shed.

He'd fetched a fallen branch from the lawn and slashed at the briar like an explorer using a machete to cut through the jungle but with little success: he'd push one cane out of the way, but as it was tangled with dozens around it, he only managed to pull more canes into his path. He then tried to open a tunnel under the canes but with even less success. Enraged, he'd struck wildly at the canes, trying to break through by sheer brute force. Now he was a medieval knight slashing at an imaginary enemy army. But the harder he hit, the further the branch bounced off the thicker canes, and even when he'd managed to flatten the thinner ones, they'd spring back towards him, imbedding their spines into his coat.

He'd given a little cry of pained surprise when one of the spines had gone through one of his mittens and punctured the skin of his finger. Wounded, he retreated back to the lawn. He pulled off his glove and rubbed the scratch. A tiny drop of bright-red blood pooled on the surface of his skin. He watched it for a second before licking it off.

It had started to rain, and, on cue, his mother had appeared at the back door. "Daniel!" she called. "You'll catch a chill. I'm not having you miss the first day at your new school. Come in at once."

* * *

The Sunday afternoon row was getting worse. His parents were moving from room to room, slamming doors as they went, their voices full of accusations and recriminations.

"I never wanted to move..." he heard his mother say.

And his father, "Daniel..." and "... better than that tiny, miserable flat!"

His parents always rowed about him, but not, he suspected, because they really cared for him. They merely used him to get at one another, alternately praising and belittling him depending on how much hurt they wanted to inflict on one another. They never considered how their comments made him feel. He tried to concentrate on the movie, wishing again that Hagrid might turn up outside the house that day to take him away. He didn't really care where to, just away from here and them.

They were a crash of broken crockery and a moment of silence before they began arguing again.

Daniel couldn't bear it any longer. He ran downstairs and stopped in the doorway to the living room where his parents were currently facing off. The argument had moved to how much time his father spent in town during the week and how convenient it was for him that they were now in the suburbs. He replied that he'd only be too pleased if she'd rather he stayed at home and she went to work eighteen hours a day so they could clothe, feed and educate *her* son. Daniel was inevitably the other parent's child in their arguments.

"Stop it!" Daniel screamed. "Stop it! Why are you always arguing? I'm hate it! And I hate you!"

The couple stared at their son, shocked into silence. Daniel turned and ran along the hall into the kitchen. Determined to get out of the house and as far away from his parents as possible, he flung open the back door.

"Come back here this minute!" Jeff shouted after him.

"Daniel!" Caroline called out.

Daniel hesitated and almost turned back. Although why he should be the one to get punished for stating the obvious, was beyond him.

"*Run outside, Daniel,*" said a voice that wasn't his own but that issued from his mouth. "*Serve them right if you slipped, hurt yourself and died,*" it cajoled. When he still hesitated at the door, it screeched, "*Run!*" This time, he was unable to resist.

The two steps down from the kitchen into the garden were wet from the rain and slippery. The smooth soles of Daniel's slippers gave him no purchase, and he lost his footing. He flailed with his outstretched arms, desperately trying to regain his balance, throwing his weight forward then backward. For a moment, he hung in mid-air, time frozen, until gravity asserted itself, and he fell headfirst towards the flagstone path.

– 2 –

The Ice Desert

Daniel slips and falls headfirst onto the path's second flagstone, which, lifted by an invasive tussock of grass, is tilted just at the right angle to cut a deep gash into his forehead. Blood oozes from the wound, soaking into the moss and grass, dyeing them a dark crimson brown.

Ouch! He thinks. That hurts! Or rather, it should hurt, but strangely, though there is pain, it doesn't feel connected to him. As a rule, he's no good with pain. When he was small, he used to cry at the slightest knock or fall, which was when his father started to get annoyed and his mother started fussing over him. Light and sound are draining from the world. Am I dying? he asks himself. Serve them right if I died. He sits up, although there doesn't seem to be any ground below him to sit on. I must be dead, he thinks.

"You're not dead," a voice says. He turns around to see Hermione floating a few feet away from him. "Well, are you just going to sit there feeling sorry for yourself?" she says, annoyed, just as if she were telling Ron or Harry off for being particularly dense.

"I could be dying," Daniel says.

"Of course, you're not dying!" She sounds like his form teacher, Mrs Johnson, who employs that tone of voice when she thinks that you're not doing your best. "Now pay attention," Hermione says more gravely. "You have to do."

"What can I do? I'm just this stupid kid who gets everything wrong," he says.

"Do you really believe that?" Her tone indicates that she's not going to fall for self-pity, real or affected.

I don't, he thinks. But my parents do.

"Ah, parents…" Hermione says, even though he hadn't spoken out loud. "They have a lot to answer for."

"Excuse me, but where am I?" he asks. He was in the garden, wasn't he? And he'd slipped on the steps and fallen over. But now he's not quite sure anymore.

"You're between nowhere and somewhere," she replies mysteriously.

"Don't you ever give answers that make sense?" Daniel asks.

"Answers make sense depending on the way you hear at them," she says. "But what's important is that soon you'll have a lot of choices to make. Make sure you make the right ones."

"What do you mean? What choices? And what are the right ones?" he asks. Silence. Come to that, he thinks, what are the wrong ones? "Hello?" he says. The silence envelops him, and with it comes the knowledge that he is quite alone. He feels the weakest of ghostly tugs, which seem to loosen the tethers that keep him anchored to the non-ground. His body begins to drift, not upwards but downwards. Oh, great, he thinks. Any minute now I'm going to see a white rabbit wearing a jacket and carrying a pocket watch. But the downward journey is featureless and completely devoid of rabbits. He has no points of reference to work out how long he's been falling for or how far when he comes to a sudden halt. One moment he's falling, the next, he's lying on a freezing-cold surface. His forehead aches, but much worse is the cold that sets his teeth chattering. He sits up and looks around. He discerns the faintest glimmer straight ahead.

"Hello," he calls out. The wind whips away his words. "Hello? Are you there?" he tries again, hoping for the reassurance of Hermione, but there's no one here, wherever here might be. He reaches up with his hand to his forehead, but there is no trace of a wound or blood. If he were Alice landing in Wonderland or one of those children who'd reached Narnia through a wardrobe, he'd say something like, "Isn't this so very strange?" But they were properly dressed for their adventures, with sensible boots and fur coats that someone had thoughtfully left in the wardrobe. Harry Potter was usually in jeans and a t-shirt, but then he had Hermione and her magic bag that always contained exactly what they needed for any adventure. Uncanny that. He's in trackie bottoms, t-shirt and slippers. Silly of him not to have worn his Wellies, mittens and winter coat.

What would Harry do? he asks himself. Teleport out of here, or never be here in the first place. "*Portus,*" he murmurs hopelessly, and, just as he'd thought, nothing happens. I'm just a muggle boy who can't do magic, he thinks bitterly. Where am I? And how did I get here? he asks himself. He was in the garden, wasn't he? He's having trouble remembering things. His parents, his teacher, Hermione... he can't quite recall who they are, and who's real and who's imaginary. The intense cold snaps him out of his reverie.

    The ground, he discovers when he tries to stand up, is covered with a thick coating of ice and snow. The thin soles of his slippers give him no purchase on the slippery surface. And as for the cold... flurries of ice crystals are whipped around him by gusts of wind. He tries to remember where he is and how he got there, but his memory only yields scattered sights and sounds that fade as soon as he tries to focus on them. The cold interrupts his mental efforts and forces him to stand up, which he succeeds in doing at his third bottom-bruising attempt. He wraps his arms around himself trying to preserve his body heat and begins to walk towards the distant pinprick of light.

* * *

Daniel lay quite still on the path, blood oozing from the gash on his forehead.

He couldn't hear his father's angry voice calling from the house, "How dare you speak to me like that? Get back here at once!"

"Daniel!" his mother called out, more concerned than angry.

"See what your constant nagging has led to!" Jeff said. And for a moment it seemed that their argument would begin again, this time about who was to blame for Daniel's uncharacteristic outburst.

But when they heard nothing from the garden, and the usually obedient Daniel had not come back to be scolded, his mother ran to the back door, imagining the worst. For once, however, her worst fears were confirmed. When she saw him lying on the path, she ran over to him and screamed, "Oh, my god! Daniel, tell Mummy where it hurts… Daniel! Daniel!"

She hovered over him, uncertain about what to do next. She wanted to scoop him up and hold him tightly in her arms, but common sense told her that an injured person shouldn't be moved, especially one with a head injury. She could see the blood pooling on the flagstone. Her husband was standing by the back door, his anger draining from him, still too shocked to speak.

Caroline was the first to unfreeze. "For god's sake, Jeff," she shouted, "don't just stand there! Call an ambulance!"

* * *

Impossibly small and far away, the tiny arctic sun creeps over the horizon, washing the snowy landscape in the feeblest of grey twilights. Daniel scans his surroundings for any sign of shelter or life. In every direction, he sees a barren wilderness of ice and snow. But as it gets a little lighter, he can make out great dark brooding shapes, scattered at intervals across the plain, rising from the mists, but they're still many cold weary steps away. There isn't enough light yet for him to tell whether they're natural features or buildings. But as they are his only hope for help or shelter, he begins to walk towards them, his arms clamped around his body to preserve as much heat as he can against the icy wind.

He's halfway to his goal when he realises that its angular outline cannot be that of a hill. It has to be a made thing – a building or group of buildings. The image of a walled city comes to into his head. He can visualise it clearly. He sees warriors in armour and plumed helmets, carrying spears, bows shields and swords on top of the crenelated battlements; the flags and banners flying from the hundreds of towers within the walls; the moat with its brackish green waters; the great gatehouse with a portcullis and drawbridge. The image is fleeting but extremely vivid. He wonders if the city he sees is home. Is he one of the warriors who guards its walls? He takes heart. If it is indeed his home, he'll soon find shelter from the numbing, icy wind.

Before long, he comes upon a broad rutted track that leads towards the city. This new sign of life cheers him, even though the road's deeply cracked surface shows no sign of recent use. He begins to run, waving his arms and calling out, "Hello! Hello!"

The road dips, and he loses sight of the city for a moment. He runs faster and crests a low hill. The city reappears. It's much closer now. But even in the grey light, he can see that what was once a great moated, walled city, whose massive outer ramparts encircle hundreds of towers, lies in ruins. The towers are gutted stumps and the walls breached, just as if a giant had brought his fists down on them; the drawbridge is smashed, its broken chains sway in the wind, clanking when they hit the crumbling masonry of the portcullis; the moat is choked with debris. Every few minutes, a loose block of masonry falls from one of the ruined towers, or a section of wall collapses, sending a cloud of ice and dust into the air.

There's no shelter here, he thinks, but what would be for the best: to freeze to death outside or be crushed by a falling building inside? He shelters behind a large piece of fallen masonry and begins to sob quietly. The cold, which he had forgotten in the excitement of finding the city, redoubles his misery. I'm lost, he thinks. I'm alone. I don't know where I am, or even who I am. He struggles again, trying to scan his memory for an explanation of how he got here. He's scared when the fleeting images of people and places yields nothing solid. He can't even remember his own name!

All of a sudden, the wind drops, and with it all sound from the city ceases with it. For a few minutes there is absolutely no sound. Then from the plain behind him comes a strange, stifling stillness that he can almost hear and feel.

"Is anybody there?" he calls out.

"Iiiiiiiiiaaaaaaaaammmmmmheeeeeeeeeeeerrrrrrrrrrrreeeeee..." It's not so much a voice, more like the soughing of the wind through dry frozen branches.

"Hello? Who are you?" he asks.

He waits for a reply, but no sound comes out of the greyness. He thinks he's imagined the strange sighing voice and returns to the problem of what to do next, but a few seconds later, he hears the eerie voice once more.

"Iiiiiiiiaaaaaaaaammmmmthththththththththhth eeeeeeeeLllllllllleeeeeeeethththththththeeeeeeeeee.... Yyyyyyyyyooooooooooouuuuuuuuuuuumuuuuuuuu uuuuuuuusssssssstSssssssssssslllllllllllleeeeeeeeppppp pp...."

Daniel peers over his makeshift shelter to see a thick white mist spreading lazily over the plain, smothering the landscape, like double cream flowing over a plate. Shapes swirl and rear up, as if the wind were whipping the mist up, but the air is completely still. Daniel thinks he can make out a figure, hands outstretched coming towards him, beckoning him into its frozen embrace: "Yyyyyyyyooooooouuuuuuuuuu muuuuuuuuuuuuuuusssssssstSsssssssssssllllllllllllll eeeeeeepppppppp...."

The voice is insistent, but there is something else... surprise, concern, maybe anger, or all three. This is no time to be awake, the sighing voice says reproachfully. Look around you, the world is in ruin, the sun is a minute teardrop of light in the darkened sky. Much better to sleep now, to sleep... sleep....

Whether it is instinct or some shred of memory forcing its way through in a time of imminent danger, he knows that he must fear this mist – the Lethe – as it comes to enfold him into its frozen embrace. If he yields to it, he may never wake up. He stares, mesmerized by the approaching cloud of whiteness. One part of him tells him to run into the city and climb into one of the towers to escape the Lethe's reach, but another is too tired and miserable to run away. Stay here, he tells himself. There's no help for you in the city, there's no help for you anywhere. You might as well give up now and sleep. No! the other voice chides. Run! There may not be help here, but the builders of the city must be somewhere. Surely, they can't all have died or left. They may just be hiding out!

The Lethe is getting closer and closer, splitting the wooden beams and stones, turning them into frozen dust as it passes over them. It is inches away from Daniel when it hesitates, like a predator faced with an unaccustomed prey. It approaches with caution and darts towards his outstretched foot.

* * *

The ambulance crew fitted Daniel with a neck brace before lifting him onto the stretcher. His mother was with him in the ambulance for the fifteen-minute drive to the local hospital, while his father followed in the car. When they'd reached the emergency department, Daniel hadn't yet regained consciousness. He was rushed down to the Imaging Department.

"He has a cranial fracture," the doctor explained to Caroline and Jeff, pointing to a jagged white line on the X-ray of Daniel's skull. "Fluid is building up here, and the pressure could become dangerous. We'll have to perform a trepanation - drill a tiny hole in his skull to let the fluid out. It's a very simple procedure and quite safe," he added.

"I have private insurance, you know, full cover," Jeff said. "I want the best for him, do you understand? The best money can buy: the best specialists, a private room, a telephone and a television."

The doctor looked impatiently past him. "Nurse, we'll be taking him straight to theatre," he said, and turning to Daniel's parents, "Now, if you'll go to reception, there are forms you have to fill in. The nurse will come and fetch you once he's out of surgery."

Two hours later, Daniel was in the private room with the telephone and television that his father's private medical insurance had paid for. His head was wrapped in a thick white bandage, and he had a tube taped into his nostril, electrodes on his chest, linked to a set of monitors on one side of the bed, and an IV in his arm.

The doctor studied a second X-ray of Daniel's skull taken after the operation, and then opened

Daniel's eyes one at a time to shine a light into his pupils. "There doesn't appear to be any damage," he said, "but he's in a coma. It's not an uncommon reaction with this kind of cranial injury. We'll have to keep him here until he regains consciousness."

"How long will that be, doctor?" his mother asked.

"It's impossible to say," the doctor replied. "Anything from a few hours to a few days."

"A few days!" his father repeated, shocked. "But what about his schoolwork?"

Again, the doctor ignored him, preferring to talk to Caroline. "I don't wish to alarm you unnecessarily, but I think you should be aware that in a very small number of cases, what seems to be a minor external injury to the skull can cause more serious internal damage to the brain, sometimes leading to impaired brain function."

"You mean he could turn out to be a vegetable," Daniel's father said callously.

"Jeff! This is our son you're talking about!" Caroline reproached him.

"Well, if you hadn't been nagging me about moving to the suburbs, this would never have happened," Jeff said angrily.

"Oh, I see, I'm to blame for everything, am I?" Caroline replied.

They were facing up for a reprise of their earlier row.

"Will you be quiet!" the exasperated doctor said. The stunned couple looked around. "You're in hospital, in your son's sickroom. If you want to argue, I'd be obliged if you waited until you were outside so that you don't disturb any of the other patients." He held the door open for them. "Reception will tell you about the facilities for overnight stays and visiting hours."

Daniel's father was about to say something, but his wife took him firmly by the arm and led him out of the room. The doctor shut the door behind them.

The City of Fallen Towers

The touch of the Lethe is so cold that it burns Daniel's foot through the sole of his slipper. He screams in pain and scrambles away from it as fast as he can. The Lethe's bite is worse than any pain he's ever experienced – although, he has no other memories of pain, he realises. The Lethe lazily smothers the fallen masonry block behind which Daniel had sheltered with a new coating of ice and sets off in pursuit.

Unnoticed by Daniel in his flight from the Lethe, the sun has crept up in the sky and fractionally gained in light and warmth. It's still too weak to melt the ice and snow smothering the plain, but it's turned the sky a perceptively lighter shade of steel-grey and made the ice stalactites that hang from the gutted towers sparkle with an inner blue fire.

Daniel run across the moat, scurrying over the debris that chokes it, concentrating hard not to lose his footing. He climbs through one of the breaches in the outer wall, which was once thick enough to contain entire suites of rooms. All that remains of the upper floors and crenelated walkways from where the defenders of the city looked out over the plain is truncated staircases and gutted rooms open to the elements.

His flight disturbs the ruins, and more than once he has to jump out of the way of a collapsing building. He turns and looks across the moat, but the Lethe is nowhere to be seen. He stops and listens and hears the stones crack and fall, but the sounds seem to be far behind him. For the first time he can examine his surroundings. He's deep within the city proper. It was once a place of great circular towers, most of which have been reduced to broken stumps and heaps of stone and masonry, but a few still stand several floors high. He counts ten surviving floors in one tower. From the quantity of debris that clogs the streets, he guesses the towers must have reached much greater heights, soaring high into the air above the outer ramparts of the city.

Although the lower portions of the walls of the towers are buried by fallen masonry, higher up, Daniel can make out decorations carved in bas-relief on the walls of the upper floors. He studies a half-buried panel, framed by an elaborate geometric border, which depicts a man is shown in profile seated on a throne. He holds a long rod in one hand and wears a high domed crown. A group of men stand before him, heads bowed, holding their fingers to their mouths in salutation. Looking more closely at the debris on the ground, he sees that much of it is decorated with intricate geometric patterns, and from the surviving traces of colour, he guesses the panels and borders were once brightly painted.

Who are they? he asks himself. Are they my people? The carvings seem both familiar and alien –

like something he's seen somewhere before – if only he could remember where. He brushes away the dust and ice from a panel. There is the same regal figure, standing this time, with a line of warriors in front of him. Another figure stands directly behind him, also wearing armour and a helmet, but it's much shorter and slighter in build. It doesn't carry a spear or sword like the other warriors but what looks like a tree branch, whose leaves have been delicately carved and still show traces of green pigment.

A sudden crash behind him makes him jump. The Lethe has found him. It unwinds its misty tentacles towards him.

"Yyyyyyyyyyyyyoooooooooooooooooouuuuuuu uuuuuuuummmmmmmmmmmuuuuuuuuuuuuuuuuus sssssssssssssssssssttttttttttttttttttsssssssssssssslllllllllllee eeeeeeeepppppppp...ssssssssssssssssslllllllllllllleeeeee eeepppppppppppppp...." It insinuates itself into his mind, trying to make him stop, to accept that he must not run away but lie down. But Daniel is wide awake now and much stronger.

"No!" he screams defiantly. He runs for cover along what must have been a broad avenue, scrambling around and sometimes over huge piles of fallen masonry. Directly ahead is a tower so large that it might hold ten of the smaller ones he's just run past. Its walls are so massive that a dozen or so of its floors are intact. Its elaborate carved gateway, though cracked and sagging, is unobstructed. Although, of the two statues that once guarded the entrance, only the legs and feet remain of one and the empty pedestal of the other. He runs in, relieved to find shelter at last. The walls glitter with ice that reflects the feeble sunlight coming from the opening in the ceiling, directly above a similar circular opening in the floor. Daniel peers down over the edge. Sniffing the air that rises from the darkness, he swears that it feels warmer than the air in the hall. He catches the faintest trace of half-remembered smells. But, as before, the images flash by so quickly that he can't hold onto them. Wet soil and grass? Rotting leaves? Compost? Words and images tumble through his mind and are gone, leaving him more puzzled than before.

He considers the well as a place to escape the Lethe and remembers another fall – and, for some reason, a white rabbit wearing a jacket and carrying a gold pocket watch. No, he thinks, I'm not going jump in and find myself in a kingdom full of weird talking animals. Where had that thought come from? If I jump in, he thinks grimly. I'll go splat at the bottom, and that will be that.

He looks around the hall. Ice has turned the floor into a glittering pavement and has coated the panels that decorate the walls and pillars. He spots the seated king once more; only here, a whole procession of men and women are paying him homage and bringing him gifts. Daniel follows the curved wall and discovers dozens of new scenes: processions, fortified camps, armies marching, in battle, besieging cities and fortresses. And here and there, the figure of the much smaller, slighter warrior who carries a branch, which is sometimes covered in leaves and sometimes covered in flowers.

Crack! The Lethe has reached the entrance of the tower. He's less frightened of it than when he first encountered it, because, though it's persistent, he's managed to outrun it so far. It fills the doorway, spilling over the door-jam. He circles the wall, searching for another way out, but the passages leading out from the hall are all blocked by fallen masonry.

Soon, most the floor is filled with the advancing Lethe. It closes in on Daniel from both right and left, forcing him ever closer to the edge of the central well. This time there's no escape. He'll be frozen on the spot or forced into the well and fall to his death. He stands as close to the edge as he dares.

"*Portus*!" he shouts, hoping against hope that the half-remembered spell will carry him to safety. He's not at all surprised when he's not magically teleported from danger. The weakened edge of the well creaks ominously under his weight and suddenly gives way. He drops into the void. He tries to grab hold of the crumbling edge, but his fingers cannot gain any purchase on the icy surface. He loses his grip and falls.

* * *

It had been three days since Daniel's surgery, but he had not regained consciousness. The specialist had been in to see him every morning and evening, and now Daniel had been taken to the hospital's medical imaging department for a full CAT scan.

Caroline was disturbed by the noisy, rotating drum of the scanner. Instinctively suspicious of technology, she also wanted whatever was best for her son. She stared at the patterns of blues, greens, reds and yellows on the screen, seeking in the sliced images of Daniel's brain something that she might identify as good or bad, but the images were totally baffling. The doctor and technician conferred over the screen.

"How is he?" she asked, unable to bear her exclusion a moment longer.

The doctor looked up, as if he were noticing her presence for the first time. "A very healthy boy," he said encouragingly. "What I find interesting are these areas here." He pointed to two bright yellow and orange patches close to the front of Daniel's skull. "The bright colours mean that we are recording quite high levels of brain activity in his frontal lobes, but this is only usually the case when someone is awake and fully conscious."

Daniel, his mother knew, was not responding to even the most basic of stimuli. She managed to look encouraged and worried at the same time.

"His brain is active and seems to be functioning normally," the doctor went on. "And there is no obvious cause for his present comatose state. Most puzzling...."

Caroline listened in a daze. As she followed the trolley from the imaging department back to Daniel's room, she wondered what had happened to her life. She'd got married, that's what had happened. But blaming it all on Jeff was a bit too easy, wasn't it? Her single-parenting mother, who'd never said she disapproved of Jeff but so obviously did; her grandmother, who'd joined the Women's Peace Camp at Greenham Common, burned her bra outside the LSE and assaulted a policeman in Grosvenor Square, had despaired of her granddaughter, who after reading English at uni, had moved to a flat share in Stoke Newington after getting a job as an editor for Everbright Books. OK, they did craft and cookery books, which weren't going to overthrow the patriarchy, but she did her bit: she voted Green and supported Extinction Rebellion on Twitter, Instagram and Facebook.

A few months later, she'd met Jeff. She was lonely in the most crowded place she'd ever lived in and so was he. He'd just started a job in finance, in pensions, which she'd thought were more acceptable than merchant banking or the stock market, not realising that pensions used merchant banks to invest in the stock market. Another few months down the line, and they'd got married in a civil ceremony, with a few friends in attendance and without parents and family. That had put her relationship with her mother and grandmother and Jeff's parents into a deep freeze that had only thawed at the birth of Daniel the following year.

The trolley was wheeled into a lift. Caroline leaned back against the cool stainless-steel panelling and closed her eyes.

"Are you just going to stand there and feel sorry for yourself," a familiar accented voice asked her. Caroline opened her eyes. The nurse accompanying Daniel had turned into Greta Thunberg. "Your house in on fire, and all you can do is play the victim." Greta was angry.

Next, the orderly spoke. When he turned to look at her, Caroline could see that it was Sir David Attenborough. "It's not too late," he said. "If we act now, we can still make a difference."

Caroline was too shocked to reply.

They looked solemnly at her and said in unison, "The Soul of the World bids you act before it's too late."

There was a ping as the door opened. Daniel was wheeled out. Caroline stayed in the lift, wondering if she'd gone mad.

"This is our floor," the now no-longer-Greta-Thunberg nurse said to her. The now no-longer-Sir-David-Attenborough orderly didn't give her a second look. He was already halfway down the corridor when she and the nurse caught up with him.

– 4 –

The Crystal Cavern

Daniel's fall is a lot shorter than he feared, but his landing is hard enough to knock the air out of his lungs. He lies on his back, gasping for breath. The floor he's landed on feels solid enough to bear his weight – at least for the time being. The rim of the well is at least six feet above. When intact, it had an overhang so that when Daniel had looked down, he couldn't see the ledge onto which he'd landed when the rim had given way. He was lucky that the rim had caved in, because had he been forced to jump, he would have fallen past the ledge and down into the abyss.

From his new vantage point, he can see that the ledge is one of many balconies that opens onto the well on the floors above. The tower's core is hollow allowing the feeble daylight to stream in. He gets up onto his hands and knees, carefully crawls over to the edge and peers down. Deep the depths, he is sure that he can make out a tiny pinprick of light. He picks up a piece of masonry and drops it into the well, but he waits in vain to hear it land.

He suddenly remembers the Lethe and looks up, half expecting it to see it come creeping down into the well, but the mist hangs above him, just visible over the edge. He picks up another piece of masonry and hurls it upwards. It explodes into fragments as it is swallowed by the freezing mist, which seems unwilling or unable to follow him. He bursts out laughing, but his relief is only temporary. He may be safe for the time being because the Lethe cannot come down, but nor can he get back to the surface. He looks for another way out, and, as his eyes become accustomed to the darkness, he makes out a large circular opening. He walks carefully towards it, testing the floor before he takes a step.

Looking around, he sees that the underground part of the tower is mostly undamaged. Any debris here has fallen down from the surface. He notices the smell again – earthy, humid…. Still only a suggestion, but it is somehow familiar: the smell of vegetation? And, the air, too, he's sure, is a little bit warmer than the icy chill of the surface. He walks through the opening and into the tunnel beyond, but because it's pitch black, he has to keep one hand on the wall to guide himself. The surface is free of ice and feels slightly damp to the touch. He can feel raised patterns under the skin of his fingers, which he thinks must be carved panels just like those he'd seen in the city above.

* * *

Jeff was waiting in Daniel's room when the orderly and nurse brought him back from his scan, with Caroline bringing up the rear. She was surprised but pleased to see him make the effort to visit during working hours. He seemed embarrassed to be there, as if showing concern for his son were somehow not the manly thing to do.

He remembered his own father's visit to him in hospital almost three decades earlier. Jeff had woken up in the middle of the night with a terrible pain in his side and a high temperature, but he knew better than to complain. He would have to be at death's door before his father would say anything else than "Don't be such a sissy, Jeff." If his mother intervened, it only made matters worse. "Don't molly-coddle the boy! Do you want to turn him into a big girl's blouse?" Dan senior would say, cutting off any further argument. His parents must have loved one another, Jeff thought. They'd stayed together for over fifty years until his mother's death, but they'd never shown it in front of other people – not even him. His father was always strict, and his mother was always deferential and quiet.

"Just do what your father says," she'd say if he appealed to her, even when his father had been in the wrong.

Of course, that time, Jeff had been at death's door. He'd had appendicitis. He'd fainted at school from the pain and had been rushed to hospital with peritonitis. It had been the talk of the class until the end of term. Even then, he remembered bitterly, he couldn't remember a single word of comfort from his father. Dan senior had come once to visit him in the crowded children's ward. Stiff and unbending in his suit, while his mother fussed with tissues, flowers, grapes and sweets. He hadn't said a word, just looked at him stone-faced, as if he were mortified that his son could be such a weakling as to need hospital treatment. And now, he could see that he'd become just like his father. He wished he'd come at another time when his wife wasn't there. He looked down at the frail little boy on the bed and saw the same unloved son that he had once been.

"They just took him down for a scan," Caroline said. He looked expectantly at her. "Oh, I didn't understand much about what they said. The doctor said there was activity in his brain, but that it wasn't normal." He looked exasperated at her. "You'd better ask him yourself," she said.

They were quiet for a moment. She was desperate to hug him, to borrow some of his apparent calmness and strength. To hear him say that everything would be alright. But he stood resolutely closed to her on the other side of the bed.

"Oh, Jeff, what would we do if he woke up... you know..." she could not bring herself to say any more.

"Disabled?" Jeff said.

"Don't...."

"Well, we'd have to be realistic!" He was almost shouting, trying to deal with the emotion the memory of his own time in hospital had brought back. "I suppose they have places for people like that," he said. He immediately regretted his own callousness.

"People like that!? You'd do that to your own son?" She said shocked, and with a pleading tone in her voice.

"Wouldn't it be for the best?" he asked, but he, too, was horrified by what he was saying.

"The best for who? For you or him?" She edged away. "How could say such a thing?" She turned her back on him and ran out of the room sobbing.

Jeff was left alone with his son. He stroked his forehead. "You'll get better, won't you, son?" But there was a sudden desolation in his voice that his usual reserve couldn't mask.

* * *

The floor of the tunnel feels solid enough. It slopes down, sometimes intersecting with other passages and stairwells that lead back upwards when he investigates them. Daniel ignores them, certain that he must go downwards where the Lethe dare not or cannot follow him, where there might be warmth and maybe even life.

Now no longer frozen or pursued by the Lethe, Daniel can focus on where he is and how he got there. But whenever he latches onto a memory, it's confused and fragmented. There was a girl – Hermione might be her name – who had told him something important about someone's eyes, and a boy, or maybe two, who had also spoken to him. He can also recall a man and a woman shouting at one another and at him. But the more he probes, the more uncertain he becomes. The tunnel, now cut off from the feeble illumination from the surface, is pitch black. I'm afraid of the dark, he thinks. Am I? he asks himself. It's pitch black here, but he's not afraid. What he's afraid of is up there, in the light.

He's still trying to remember who he is and where he's from when he catches sight of the faintest glow issuing from the darkness ahead. It's not the grey surface light but a watery, blue-green glow. After another ten minutes, the glow is just about bright enough to illuminate the tunnel. He can make out the painted carvings that cover the walls from floor to ceiling. The panels are bordered by interlaced circles, squares and triangles and garlanded with snaking loops and lines, just like those he saw in the upper city.

The people depicted are now familiar: the seated man, flanked by his attendants, courtiers and warriors standing stiffly around him. Unlike those in the ruins above, the carvings here are undamaged, and as the glow grows in intensity, he can make out their bright colours. The air has become warmer and damper, too. Water droplets condense on the walls and drip from the ceiling. A thin film of algae grows over the upper portions of the panels.

He turns a corner and comes to a huge archway many times his own height – the source of the blue-green glow. He takes a deep breath and steps forwards. What he sees makes him dizzy. He's standing at the very top of a steep staircase overlooking a vast bowl-shaped cavern, so wide that an identical opening opposite appears no larger than one of his fingernails.

Apart from the circular opening in the centre of the ceiling, which Daniel guesses to be the same well that leads all the way up to the surface far above, every available inch of floor space is covered with large blue and green crystals, like giant emeralds and sapphires. Now he understands what caused the glow in the tunnel. The well allows a tiny amount of light from the surface into the giant cavern, where it is picked up and reflected by the crystals, whose individual glow is faint, but which together flood the whole space with an eerie, watery luminescence. The crystals are arranged in a spiral pattern that starts on the upper slopes of the cavern and ends in the middle of the floor beneath, in a circle of fourteen crystals evenly spaced around what looks like a large circular white stone table.

He descends the staircase, soon losing sight of the cavern behind the crystals, which grow out of the rock slopes and tower above him. He wants to inspect them more closely, but a deep channel separates them from the stairway. He starts to run, taking two or three steps at a time, concentrating hard on his feet so as not to trip and fall.

"*Don't go so fast, Daniel. You'll only fall and hurt yourself,*" he hears a woman's voice say in his head. "*Oh, look what's happened now! I told you so!*" The voice goes on.

But then an angry man's voice intervenes: "*Cry baby! You're so clumsy! Pick yourself up and stop crying!*"

He slows and stops. He knows the voices so well, but he can't remember who they belong to. Emotions well up from deep within –fear, frustration and anger. But the memory fades and is gone before Daniel has a chance to examine it further. The gradient of the stair gradually reduces, and the steps become longer and shallower.

The spiral stair leads to the centre of the cavern, to the edge of what he had thought was a round stone table but turns out to be a pool of frozen water that is the same size as the opening in the cavern roof. The last fourteen crystals are not packed closely together like the others but are spaced at regular intervals around the pool. He approaches one of the crystals to study it more closely. The surface is clouded with condensation. He rubs it gently with his hand. The warmth of his fingers instantly clears the condensation on the crystal's surface. He looks inside, and a fierce, frowning face stares straight back at him. He screams and jumps back.

The face belongs to a warrior wearing a high-crested helmet. His eyes are open, but Daniel realises that the face with its frightening expression is painted on the face plate of the helmet. He wears a tunic made of silver lozenges and a dark green cloak over his shoulders that reaches down to the floor. He is arm with a sword, spear and a round shield. Daniel realises with some relief that the warrior within the crystal cannot see or hear him, because he is frozen in sleep or death.

Daniel moves to the next crystal and presses his fingers against it, again instantly clearing the fog of condensation. Its occupant is an old man dressed in a long black robe and carrying a staff. He wears no silver tunic or helmet, and his eyes are shut. But when he reaches the third crystal, which is slightly larger than the others, the figure he sees inside wears a high, domed crown, just like the carvings of the seated man he has seen on the panels. He carries a long golden rod – a sceptre – in one hand, while the other rests on the hilt of a golden sword studded with gems.

When he looks into the next crystal, he thinks it is just another warrior in helmet and armour, but instead of a spear and shield, the figure carries a green branch covered in leaves, as fresh and green as they would be in springtime. He looks more closely at the warrior's visor and realises that the face painted on it is that of a young girl with green-on-green eyes with gold-flecked irises. *Look for one with green-on-green eyes*, he remembers someone telling him, but who was it?

* * *

With Daniel in hospital, Caroline had missed her weekly visit to see Dan senior. She hadn't even thought of phoning him to tell him about Daniel's accident. She knew Jeff wouldn't have done either, because even during Dan senior's illness, he'd delegated his father's care to her. Jeff saw his father as little as possible, now only on the obligatory family holiday visits, when she insisted that he make the effort. Father and son were not estranged, as far as she knew. There was no talk of a blistering family row to explain why they had so little to do with one another. Like father, like son, she thought sadly. It was the main reason she'd tried to influence Daniel's development – to undo the malign influence of two generations of male emotional cripples.

She dialled the number of the nursing home and got through to reception. They'd given Dan senior a mobile, but he forgot to charge it, and whenever she visited, she invariably found it abandoned on the bedside table. Fortunately, he also had a landline in his room connected to reception. It was like calling into the past. The ring tone, and brisk voice of the receptionist at the other end. "Meadow Vale nursing home," the receptionist would say, before putting her through to Dan senior's room, where she imagined he'd be sitting stiffly in jacket, shirt and tie, in spite of his partial paralysis.

"Hello, dad," she began. "I'm sorry about last week…." And then, she was at a loss at how to tell him about the accident. She was afraid he'd ask her how it had happened, and she'd have to admit that she and Jeff had been rowing at the time. But the old man hadn't said much. He'd asked about Daniel, but in a tone that made her think that he wasn't taking her seriously – that it was just her fussing again over some minor ailment. "He's in a coma," she said. "And they don't know when he'll wake up."

She was on the verge of tears. What was wrong with the men of the family she'd married into? When she'd met Jeff, she'd admired his emotional reserve that made him look strong and confident. If only she'd known then that what she'd thought of as strength and confidence was really the repression of feelings he didn't know how to deal with.

"I'm sure the lad will be alright," Dan senior had said vaguely and with what she took to be little real concern for Daniel's condition.

"I'll try and come to see you next week," she said anxious to end the conversation.

"Only if you have the time," he'd replied.

After she'd hung up, Dan senior picked up the little book that Daniel had given him on his last visit to the nursing home. He'd made it himself, he'd told Dan senior proudly. "I typed it all out on the computer, found images on the Internet, and printed it out."

Amazing what kids could do these days. The book was called *Wonders of the Ancient World* and was Daniel's account of the civilisations of ancient Egypt, Mesopotamia, Greece and Rome. It wasn't a list of dates of kings and battles, like the history Dan senior had studied at school, but an imaginative travelogue of reconstructed ancient cities and pictures of Greek and Egyptian statues and Persian, Babylonian and Assyrian bas-reliefs. It was a child's view of the past without all the bad stuff – wars, famines, pandemics – a grand place for a boy to have an adventure. Daniel had excitedly explained each illustration to him, naming long-dead kings and faraway places. Dan senior turned the pages carefully, as if he were afraid of damaging them with his overlarge fingers and thought about the little boy in hospital. When he'd finished leafing through the ten or so pages, there were tears in his eyes.

Invaders!

Daniel examines the frozen figures in the glittering crystals. Sarcophagi. The word seems to rise up from the depths of his memory, and with it, images of ancient Egyptian mummy cases painted, cast or carved in the likenesses of their occupants. He tries to hold on to the memory, but it slips away like the other glimpses of that other world he's now sure must be his own.

A sound at the very threshold of Daniel's hearing brings him back to the here and now.

Plop!

It's a familiar sound, like a very faint but insistent tapping. He scans the nearest crystals, but the sound isn't coming from their direction.

Plop!

He closes his eyes to help him focus on the sound.

Plop!

There it is again…. He turns slowly, holding his breath so that it does not mask the sound. Golden light fills the circular well, coming from the world far above, heralding blue skies and warm sunshine.

A flash far above catches his eye. A single drop, no larger than a tear, falls through the column of light, leaving a silver trail. It lands in the very centre of the pool, where it makes an indentation in the frozen surface. A second drop follows, then a third and a fourth, always landing in the same spot, until, after a few minutes, the hollow has become a tiny pool of meltwater.

The ice in the city above is melting, he realises. What will happen to the cavern? Will it fill up with water? His fear is not for himself but for the people inside the crystals, and especially for the girl with green-on-green eyes.

A barely noticeable shudder rises from deeper within the earth. It grows until it is it begins to make the crystals in the cavern vibrate in sympathy. A violent tremor sends Daniel tumbling to his knees. A small crystal, much smaller than those around the pool comes rolling down the slope through and crashes into the side of the ice pool. It shatters, covering the ground in brilliant fragments. Daniel picks up one of the green shards. It's not sharp like broken glass but is a perfectly shaped geometrical shape. He picks up a handful of the fragments – each one is a distinct geometric shape: pyramid, tetrahedron, octahedron, and cube, so that the crystal must have been a three-dimensional puzzle made up of thousands of the interlocking pieces.

A whimper makes carefully brush the fragments to one side. He uncovers the top of a small furry head. It is some kind of animal – a cat or dog? He remembers both these animals, but he's also sure they don't belong here.

He bends down and gently digs through the crystals, saying, "It's alright. Are you hurt?" The only answer is another faint whimper. He carefully excavates a small head with two large triangular ears and large gold-green-flecked eyes. The creature's long prehensile tail emerges from the pile and wraps itself weekly around his wrist. The creature is soft and frail and covered in gold fur with grey-green stripes. "What are you?" he asks.

He digs out the rest of the body and holds the little creature close to him. Tiny hands and prehensile feet grip onto his t-shirt. The creature's body is about six inches long with a tail as long again.

"Chirrip!" the creature squeaks, holding on more tightly as Daniel stands up. It sounds like a cross between a cat purring and a bird tweeting.

"You must have been in the crystal that rolled down," Daniel says.

"Chirrip! Chirrip!" the creature answers, as if agreeing with Daniel.

"Well, at least, you don't seem hurt."

If you were in the crystal and are now awake, he thinks. The people in the crystals must also be in some kind of sleep.

The little creature quickly gains in strength and confidence as it recovers from the fall. It clambers up from his arm onto his shoulder and wraps its tail around his neck to hold itself steady. The fur of its tail tickles his neck, and he bursts out laughing.

"What are you called?" he asks the little creature. "You can't tell me, can you? I'll call you Chirrip," he says happily.

Another tremor rocks the floor of the cavern. He steadies himself on a crystal – the girl's – which rocks alarmingly.

"Chirrip! Chirrip! Chirrip!" the little animal squeaks when he sees the occupant of the crystal.

A mighty crash on the far side of the cavern floor tells him that more crystals have come crashing down.

"We'd better get out of here!" He starts to run for the stair.

He begins the climb out of the cavern, taking the stairs as fast as he dares as tremors continue to bring down crystals all around him. Although he's climbing, he's making better time because the tunnels are now more brightly lit – from the increasing glow from the cavern, and also as a warm, yellow light makes its way down from the surface through dozens of shafts in the ceiling of the tunnels. When he comes to a fork in the tunnels and hesitates, Chirrip tugs at one of his ears, as if to tell him which path to take.

He doesn't follow the same route as before and instead of emerging below ground level on the balcony inside the well, he finds himself looking down from a gallery into the circular entrance hall of the tower. He remembers that the tower had windows in the walls of its upper floors. He climbs a rickety staircase and runs along a corridor, looking for a doorway to one of the outer rooms. Soon he comes to a door half hanging off its hinges. He pushed it open, and steps into a small room with a triangular window. He tests the floor before starting across it, but it feels solid. He walks over to the window and looks out.

He has climbed higher than the surrounding towers and overtops what remains of the city walls. The sun is a bright yellow ball, warmer now, though still low in a cloudless pale, blue-grey sky. The air is still cool but so much warmer than the frozen ground that where the two meet, the difference in temperature has created a thick layer of fog, which shrouds the city streets and the surrounding country to a height of seven or eight feet. But this fog is not like the all-smothering Lethe. It's light and is blown about by the breeze. Beyond the city walls, the once barren landscape is filled with the sounds of unseen activity.

As he scans the horizon for a clue to the cause of all this sudden noise where there was once only a barren wasteland of snow and ice, a section of the outer wall and the stumps of several neighbouring towers collapse, throwing up clouds of dust and ice. Daniel hears a distant cheer. A vision of warriors pouring through the gaps in the city's breeched defences fills his mind's eye. Invaders!

"Chirrip!" the little creature screeches in fear.

He makes his way back to the stairs and runs down to the circular entrance hall. The fog has drifted in from the street, and as soon as he exits the tower, he can see no more than a few paces in front of him.

He can hear the commotion from the direction of the new breech in the wall. People are running and shouting orders in a language that he can't understand. Whoever they are, they're making straight for him and the central tower. A gust of wind clears the fog from the street, revealing a column of foot soldiers in yellow and blue capes, with a yellow crest on their helmets, shields, lances and swords in hand, bounding over the rubble-clogged the streets. Their leader sees him at the same moment as he sees them.

"*At'illo!*" he shouts to his troops. "*At'illo Argaë!*"

The invaders are closing in fast. Daniel turns and runs back into the tower. He tries in vain to pull the double doors shut, but the entrance is clogged with too much debris. A hail of arrows and spears forces him to retreat into the tower.

The sleepers in the cavern are in danger! He must warn them. He runs down the stairs that lead into the labyrinth of underground passages under the tower. There is no green glow to guide him because the tunnels are now brightly lit from above, but Chirrip guides him again, pulling on his ears to indicate which path to take when he hesitates. At least the labyrinth of intersecting tunnels and staircases will slow the invaders down. But what can he do alone by one against so many? If only there was a way of waking the warriors asleep in the crystals.

Despite the labyrinth of passages, the invaders are close behind him. He can hear the clatter of their armour and shields, the clash of their axes, spears and swords as they scrape against the carvings on the walls. Their war cry, "*At'illo Argaë!*" reverberates through the tunnels. The clamour is so loud that, soon, Daniel can no longer tell whether they are behind or in front of him.

He almost topples forward down the stairs as he bursts into the crystal cavern. "Wake up! Invaders!" he shouts. "Wake up! They're coming!"

There's no reply. The place remains cocooned in stillness, and Daniel is relieved to see that though many crystals have fallen, the sarcophagi in the centre of the cavern are intact and standing.

They'll all be killed, he thinks. The enemy warriors are already flooding into the cavern from entrances all around the rim.

He stands in front of the girl's sarcophagus and swears to die defending her. But he has doesn't even have a weapon to fight with. The enemy is closing in. They're more interested in the crowned man than the girl. They approach with caution, forcing Daniel closer and closer to the king's sarcophagus.

The leader of the yellow and blue warriors stands over him. "*At'illo sumla Argaë!*" he bellows, raising his double headed axe ready to strike at the king.

"Noooooo!" Daniel shouts, throwing himself at the giant warrior's legs, momentarily throwing him off balance.

Instead of cleaving the king's sarcophagus in two, the axe is deflected and smashes into the crystal side on. The surface crazes and explodes. The warrior raises his axe again, this time turning his attention on Daniel. The axe blade swings down towards him, but a golden sceptre intercepts the blow in a mighty crash of sparks.

Daniel looks up to see the king, golden sceptre held at arm's length holding the enemy warrior's axe from his head. At the same moments all the crystals in the cavern explode, releasing the imprisoned warriors. Daniel blacks out.

* * *

Caroline sat by the bed, as she did most mornings and evenings. She'd taken up knitting to give her something to do during her visits. The television murmured in the background – a program that Daniel liked to watch – but she wasn't paying attention. Her needles clicked as she chatted to him as if he were awake.

"I saw Mrs Reeves today, you know, Timmy's mother. Anyway, she and Mr Reeves are—" She stopped in mid-sentence. Daniel was breathing heavily as if he were running, his whole body wracked by convulsions. The usually silent display on the monitors beside the bed had gone from a smooth curve to a jagged series of peaks that were shooting off the edges of the screen, setting off an alarm that summoned the duty nurse. She came running in, closely followed by a doctor carrying a hypodermic.

"What's happening to him?" Caroline screamed in panic.

The nurse moved her to one side, gently but firmly, as the doctor injected Daniel. The display gradually flattened and returned to normal. A few moments later the consultant arrived.

    Caroline repeated her question, but the answer she got did little to reassure her. "In twenty years of medical practice with this kind of injury, I've never seen anything like this," the consultant told her. "His brain is showing unusual signs of activity, including areas that control the motor functions of his body and his senses and yet he's in a deep coma. It's almost as if he were awake, only not here but somewhere else."

– 6 –

The New Citadel

Daniel opens his eyes and experiences a moment of uncertainty: confused images succeed one another too fast for him to focus on any one of them: a garden, a house, an icy cold plain, a ruined city, a giant cavern, warriors!

"Invaders!" he shouts. He raises his arms in front of his face, protecting himself from the killing axe blow, but all he succeeds in doing is to tangle himself in the bedclothes. He relaxes. He's in bed; the sheets are woven from fine green strands, which are unusually warm and soft. Gradually, he puts his memories of recent events into some kind of coherent order. He'd escaped the Lethe on the icy plain and found his way into the ruined city. Chased by the Lethe he'd fallen into the labyrinth of tunnels that led down to the crystals cavern. He remembers the sleeping warriors, the king and the girl, and the arrival of the invading warriors.

He untangles himself from the sheets and looks around. He's in a small chamber, its walls covered with woven hangings, with geometric designs in muted greens, yellows and browns. A curtain made of a gauze-like material billows over a triangular window, straining the light, making it look as if he were deep in a forest glade in early summer. The air is cool, but it has none of the chill of the ice desert. Everything looks new and smells fresh. But it's the noises he can hear coming from the outside world that he's keen to investigate – sawing and hammering, the rumble of carts and of people calling to one another – the sounds of life.

He swings his legs over the edge of the bed. He feels weak, and his legs almost give way as he tries to stand up. He sits back, but curiosity forces him to make a second attempt. This time he succeeds in reaching the window. He steadies himself with one hand and draws the curtain with the other.

Daniel looks down onto a city that he'd last seen in ruins but which is now a vast building site. Perched many floors above ground, he has a bird's eye view of the activity below. The city is being re-built, but not from the base of the ruined towers. Instead, the builders are starting from the highest storey that is solid enough to bear the weight of new construction. New suspended walkways have been built over the ones clogged with debris, giving access to new entrances, five, sometimes ten, floors above the former ground level. Anything cleared from the towers is cast over the walkways into the underworld below. The new suspended streets are wide enough to accommodate two loaded carts abreast, while a network of pedestrian walkways, sometimes only a few paces wide, snakes around and between the towers.

The scaffolding erected around the towers is covered in workers making good the damage to the lower floors and building new floors. The tower directly opposite grows as he watches. Carpenters assemble the spiral staircases around the light well in the centre of the tower, position the carved frames for the windows and doors, and the joists and planking for the new floor, while masons in long aprons, cut and lay the courses of stones that will be the inner and outer walls. No sooner have the carpenters and masons finished and moved up to the next floor that others bring matting for the floor and hangings for the walls like the ones that decorate his room. Around the entrance of the tower, stone carvers are at work on the panels that Daniel had seen in ruins. As soon as the sculptors are finished, the painters arrive with their paint pots and brushes to add bright splashes of colour to the streets of the new city.

He finally notices the thing that has been nagging at his attention. Why hadn't he seen of it before? The design of the towers, the carved and painted panels, the decorations within are all the same. There is no variety at all, as if there were just one model for each one. I don't come from a world where everything is so standardised, he realises. He studies the people of the city more closely and finds the same sameness. The masons and carpenters are all dressed in identical outfits, as are the sculptors and painters, who carry the same toolkits to execute the same designs.

As soon as the hangings are up in the floor opposite, new residents move in, bringing with them their goods and furniture. A boy of about his own age sticks his head out of the window. He is carrying a long piece of cloth that he unfurls over the windowsill to air. When he sees Daniel, he smiles and waves at him before going back inside. The sound of drums makes Daniel look down. A column of warriors, five abreast, their spears held aloft, is marching down the street towards one of the city gates. Again, their uniforms, helmets, armour and weapons are identical.

He looks over the city walls, now as tall and solid as when they were first built, to the plain beyond. The sky has turned a cloudless pale blue. He finds it hard to believe that this is the same barren desert across which he'd wandered frozen and lost. There's no sign of the Lethe, nor of the fog that hid the plain before the attack on the cavern. In the bright sunshine, he can see pitched battles in open areas, sieges of the new fortified camps and villages, and attempts to wreck the constructions of those who have not managed to build their defences high enough. But there are also more peaceful activities: markets, festivals and forage parties collecting water and building materials.

"Chirrip!" The small creature runs up his leg and up his back to his shoulder, nuzzling his face.

"Hello, Chirrip, where have you come from?"

"I must thank you for taking such good care of him," a voice says from the doorway. A girl steps into the room. She wears a cape of moss-green and silver threads over her silver breastplate, and instead of a helmet, she is crowned with a silver filigree circlet of hung with silver leaves studded with green gemstones.

It's the girl from the crystal cavern.

They both hesitate for a few seconds as they notice each other's eyes and try to recall something they'd been told. Hers are green-on-green with gold-flecked irises, his, pale blue, the colour of the cloudless sky over the plain.

She is the first to break the silence. "I am Eireis, Caller of the Argaë," she says, expecting him to reply in kind. He recognizes the word "Argaë" from the war cries of the invaders.

"I wish I could tell you my name, but I cannot remember anything of the time before I came here."

She studies him for a few moments and says, "You're a stranger here, that I know. I have never seen eyes such as yours...." She hesitates, probing her memory once more. "They're the colour of the sky in the second quadrant. Are you a creature of the sky? Are you an Unseen One?"

"I don't think so... I don't know...." he answers. But how does he know if he is or not? He might be.

"You must be hungry. I've had some food prepared for you," she says, signalling a woman standing by the open door to come in. She enters and places a tray on the bedside table. She takes one look at Daniel, let's out a muffled scream and scurries out of the room, closing the door behind her.

Daniel wants to ask Eireis why the woman was afraid of him, but before he can speak, she says, "Eat now. We'll talk later when you're stronger."

Daniel sits down on the bed and does not wait for any more encouragement. He gulps down the bowlful of an insubstantial golden-yellow soup that has neither taste nor texture.

At first, he'll appear weak and helpless, and you must help him. He is our hope for the future. You will know him by his sky-tinted eyes.... She remembers the words of the Unseen One, and the terrible dream-visions that had preceded them.

"It is poor stuff, I'm afraid," she says. "What was left from our stores from last Greenday."

"It's delicious," he says scraping the bowl clean.

"How do you feel?" she asks.

"Much better, thank you," he answers, straightening up to appear stronger than he feels.

One will come to you; one who will be a bridge between the worlds. At first, she'll appear strong and confident, but you must help her. She is our hope for the future. You will know her by her green-on-green eyes.... That's what Hermione, Harry and Ron had said, but what had they meant? And, of course, he'd like to remember who Hermione, Harry and Ron are. Are they friends of mine? He wonders. Probably not. Hermione was bossy, and the two boys were annoyed with him. He's glad Eireis is here and not Hermione. Even after this seemingly insubstantial meal, Daniel feels better than he has since he awoke on the icy plain. "This may sound strange," he says. "But where am I?"

Before Eireis can reply, the door is flung open.

"You are in the Citadel of the Argaë," says an old man, bursting into the room. He is tall and gaunt and has long, greying, unkempt hair. His robe is woven from green threads so dark that it looks almost black. He carries a staff of gnarled wood, which he holds out in front of him like a weapon, as if he were expecting Daniel to attack him. Daniel is struck by the contrast between the two Argaë. And what about the woman who had brought him the food. She'd been scared. The old man, too, is scared, Daniel senses, but he cloaks his fear in anger and bluster.

"This is Magrave, Keeper of the Lore," Eireis says coldly.

"Fair of shape but foul of heart!" Magrave says, making a sign with his fingers in the empty space between them. The air shimmers for a moment. "He is neither an Unseen One nor any other creature of the sky as you believe, Caller. Look at him! His eyes are sky-tinted! He is an abomination! He must be exiled from the Citadel at once!"

"That is for my father, the Archon, to decide, Lord Keeper."

"It is, indeed, Caller. I shall see you both at the Archon's Council," he says gathering his tattered robe and sweeping out of the room.

Daniel turns expectantly to Eireis.

"I fear that Margrave is right. You are a stranger not just to the Argaë but also to the Green

Kingdom. I have never seen or heard of one such as you...." Her words trail off as she half remembers something. A memory floats tantalizingly just out of reach.

She is distracted when he says, "But I mean the Argaë no harm."

"I know, but Margrave fears anything that he does not understand and cannot control. He tried his strongest spells on you, and they had no effect. I fear he will not rest until you are exiled from the Citadel or dead. But that decision is not his to make. You have done a great service to the Argaë, and I know my father will not repay you by punishing you. Come. We have been summoned to the Council. There my father, the Archon, ruler of the Argaë, will decide your fate."

* * *

Jeff was sitting in his car in the nursing home car park. He'd phoned work to tell them he wouldn't be able to make it that morning. But he was now having second thoughts about the visit. A carer came out of the front door. She helped an old lady down the front steps. They were going for a stroll in the grounds. The old woman beamed at him as they passed the car.

"Oh, hell," he murmured under his breath and got out of the car.

The lobby was decorated with fresh flowers and prints of countryside scenes. Despite the laboured attempts at cheeriness, he found the place deeply depressing.

"You're here to see Mr Daniel Graham?" the receptionist asked.

"Yes, my father."

"Of course, I'm sure he'll be so happy to see you. Do you know the way to the visitors' lounge?" The receptionist managed to insert a tone of mild reproach. He hadn't been to see his father since outside visits had been allowed again. Caroline had visited as often as she could, taking Daniel with her. He thought it strange that grandson and grandfather got on so well, while he hadn't exchanged a meaningful word with his father since his mother's death.

Dan sat upright and dressed, as ever, in jacket, shirt and tie in the lounge. A man who had never had a day's illness in his life, he'd been laid low by a heart attack followed by a stroke. Partially paralyzed on his right side, he'd lost the power of speech for several months. But he was a fighter and with physical and speech therapy, he'd now regained his speech and some mobility on his right side. The home had told them that he could leave in the next few months but that he could not live on his own. That had clinched Jeff and Caroline's move to the suburbs. The pandemic had delayed matters by almost two years, but partly at the nursing home's request, and partly because of the rising costs of Dan senior's ongoing car, Jeff and Caroline had decided it was time for the old man to move back to Greenacres.

"Hello, dad," Jeff said. "How are you keeping?"

"Get it over with lad," Dan senior began briskly. "I know why you're here. You've come to tell me you can't have two invalids at home, and that I'll have to stay here." In a strange way, Dan senior was glad he wouldn't have to go back to Greenacres where he'd feel that was an unwanted guest of the new occupiers.

"No, dad, that's not what I came here to tell you," Jeff said quickly, but he was dismayed by the thought that Dan senior took it for granted they'd rather he stayed here, out of sight and out of mind. Maybe that's how I've been treating him since mum died, he thought sadly. "I'm here to come to take you to the hospital to see Daniel. I mean if you're up to it."

"Up to it! I've never felt better. Let's go."

He still walked stiffly, leaning on a walking stick on his weaker side. He needed help to keep steady while negotiating the steps at the front door, but he'd point blank refused to walk down the ramp or be pushed the short distance to the car in a wheelchair.

* * *

"We are in the Archon's Tower," Eireis explains as they make their way down from Daniel's room. She stops at an upper gallery from where they can look down into the large circular room. "And this is the Archon's Council Chamber."

"It's just like the carvings on the walls," Daniel says excitedly.

"The Archon sits on his throne with his attendants around him," Eireis says, "in front of the Council of the people and warriors. Come, we mustn't keep father waiting." She leads the way down a staircase to a side entrance behind the Archon's throne.

An attendant is waiting for him holding an Argaë's long green cape for Daniel to wear in the Archon's presence. Eireis fastens it around his neck with a silver clasp and gives him an encouraging smile before going to her own seat slightly set back to the right of her father's throne. The attendant preceding him, Daniel is ushered in front of the throne, in full view of the assembled Argaë. A murmur rises around the chamber. They, too, have seen the colour of his eyes, which immediately sets him apart from the Argaë who, like all other tribes of the green kingdom, have green-on-green eyes.

"The supplicant will approach the throne," the attendant announces.

Daniel steps forwards and makes a deep bow and holds two fingers of his right hand to his mouth in the manner Eireis had shown him and which he himself had noticed on the carved panels decorating the towers. This makes a good first impression on the Council. Daniel notices the approving nods of the Argaë. He may be a stranger, but he is no barbarian to be condemned to death or summarily banished from the Citadel.

"Let those who will speak for and against the stranger come forwards," the Archon's chamberlain announces.

The first to speak is Magrave who has risen from one of the seats to the left of the Archon.

"I speak for the Lore." He turns and points to Daniel with his staff. "Do not be taken in by his youth, short stature and apparent weakness! This stranger is a monster from beyond the Green Kingdom. His presence here is an offence to all that we hold sacred, and his presence means doom to the Argaë! The Lore is plain: no stranger may find shelter among the Argaë. This is and has always been the Lore of the Citadel. If he is not to be killed, he must be exiled at once!" With these words, Margrave sits down. The ranks of the loremasters behind him strike the floor with their staves to mark their approval.

When the din has been silenced, the chamberlain asks, "Who will speak for the stranger?"

"I shall." Eireis steps forwards. A hush falls over the chamber and all eyes turn towards the Caller. "The Lord Keeper is right; the Lore is plain: no stranger may live amongst the Argaë. Yet, no stranger has ever done the Argaë so great a service. With a bravery that knew no care for his own life, he saved my lord father, the Archon. The stranger is lost, far from his own home in the sky. Look at his eyes, they speak plainly enough of his origins. I beg the Council's leave to help the stranger find his way home, thus the Lore will be respected and our debt of honour to him will be repaid."

It is the warriors and courtiers who now mark their approval by stamping their feet or striking their shields with the hilts of their swords.

The Archon stands up and raises his sceptre to silence the Council. "My daughter has spoken with both wisdom and honour," he says. "For your service to the Argaë, stranger, I shall give you shelter and help you find your way back home, wherever that may be. Now, stranger, kneel." With these words he draws his golden sword. He touches Daniel's shoulders lightly with the blade. "Rise, now no longer a stranger, but for as long as you are among us, a page of the Archon, and as such, under my direct protection." He looks towards Margrave and adds, "And any who try to injure you, will have to answer to me," he says sheathing his sword.

The World of the Argaë

Eireis joins Daniel, who is surrounded by a crowd of well-wishers. "Come on, stranger. Let me show you the Citadel." She doesn't give him time to answer before she leads him away.

They emerge from the Archon's Tower onto the broadest street of the Citadel, which leads to the main gate. It hugs the towers on either side so closely that it looks as if it were built on solid ground. The openings to the world below have disappeared. Although the street is wide enough to take several carts abreast, it's crowded with workmen, warriors and Argaë leading livestock and carrying provisions. There is no idleness here, Daniel notes. Everyone is doing something – even the children carry goods and run errands.

"Where did all these people come from?" Daniel asks.

"As the sun begins to set at the end of Greenday," Eireis explains, "we take shelter in the caverns deep beneath the Citadel, with all our goods and animals. We sleep within the crystals that you saw all through Whiteday, until the dawning of the new Greenday sun awakens us once more. Every tower in the city has several caverns such as the one you saw under the Archon's Tower, some for people, others for animals and stores."

"You sleep through the ice and darkness and the Lethe?"

"What?" She says, suddenly shocked. "How can you know of such things? Don't talk of them here because others will overhear us. Magrave has eyes and ears everywhere," she whispers. Her worried tone silences his many further questions. "We'll speak later in private." Then more brightly, she adds, "But now, let me show you the Citadel."

The Archon's Tower and the other buildings at the heart of the Citadel have been repaired and soar ever higher with the addition of new floors. The outer walls, too, have been rebuilt, and in some places their circuit has been enlarged to take in more land on which the foundations of new towers are being excavated. Daniel imagines that the builders are excavating passages down to caverns like the one he'd seen under the Archon's Tower.

"What is that tower?" Daniel asks. It is close to the Archon's Tower and larger in circumference at the base, but much shorter, being no more than seven floors high. The differences do not stop there. Where the Archon's Tower is brightly painted both inside and out, with a wide gateway, open to all, the carved designs on this tower's outer walls do not depict the Archon and his attendants or any scene Daniel has seen so far, but geometrical patterns in muted dark tones. Set within them are shapes that Daniel finds unsettling – faces that are not quite faces, mouths open as if screaming in anger or pain. The doorway is so low that Daniel would have to stoop to enter it, and the ancient door, unlike the open portals of all the other towers that are always open, is tightly shut.

"That is the Tower of the Lore," Eireis answers. "Within it are stored the archives of the Argaë since the beginning of the Green Kingdom. It is the domain of Margrave and the loremasters. You must promise me never to enter that tower, for to do so means instant death to any but the initiated."

"I promise," he answers, but his curiosity has been aroused. Maybe the answers he seeks are locked away in the dark passageways of Margrave's domain.

Eireis sets off down the street in the opposite direction. "Come on! Look!" she says, pointing up. "The first mirrors are being raised!"

He follows her gaze. A large circular mirror is being hauled up within a rope cradle to the summit of one of the neighbouring towers.

"What is it?" he asks.

"You really know nothing of this kingdom, do you?" she says quietly so no one can hear her. "Only ask questions of me. We Argaë are not used to strangers. You look much like one of us in your new clothes, apart from the strangeness of your sky-tinted eyes, but your ignorance sets you apart and will make them distrust and fear you."

He sees many sights with his guide that day, each more marvellous and many more mysterious than the next, but he does not dare inquire about what they are but tries to guess as best he can. They watch as a great mirror is hauled up to the summit of another tower and fixed into position. To the cheers of the spectators and workers, the mirror is turned to face the new sun, now a yellow ball halfway up in the eastern sky; it catches its rays and blazes with blinding, white fire so bright that the onlookers have to shield their eyes from the glare.

"Quick, or it will start before we get there." She beckons him to the tower's open doorway. Inside the ground-floor room, there is a smaller version of the well he saw in the Archon's Tower. It runs the whole length of the tower to the summit, now a dozen or so floors above, and Daniel guesses, many floors to a cavern far below ground. The light collected by the mirror on the tower's summit, is somehow reflected downwards through the centre of the well. There is a sudden hiss, and a column of steam shoots from below ground, followed seconds later by a column of water. The water rises slowly as if drawn upwards by the light and disappears through the hole in the ceiling and continues upwards until it reaches the top of the tower.

"The water of the earth and the warmth of the sun combine to give us everything we need," Eireis explains. "As the water rises, it give us the power for the looms to make our cloth and for the lathes to make our tools." She leads him to a niche in the wall in which there is a tap set over a small circular basin. "Hold out your hands," Eireis says. Daniel makes a cup with his hands under the tap. She turns the tap and a golden substance, not quite water and not quite light, but a mixture of the two, flows slowly out. It lands in Daniel's palm but feels neither wet nor dry. It does not seem to have any real weight or substance.

"This is our food, stranger," she explains. "We call it niktar. Drink it quickly before it evaporates. We store what we do not use in the caverns below the Citadel, to provide us with nourishment when we awake from the sleep of Whiteday."

He inhales rather than drinks the strange substance in his cupped palm, and it makes his nose, mouth and throat tingle. It has no taste he can discern, but he can feel it spreading throughout his body, nourishing and refreshing him from the inside. A queue of Argaë has formed behind them to drink from the fountain, and Eireis pulls Daniel gently aside.

As they step out into the street, Daniel sees that mirrors have been raised on the summits of all the towers of the Citadel.

* * *

"Poor little mite," Dan senior said as he walked into his grandson's hospital room. He was shocked by Daniel's pallor and stillness, and by the tubes and wires attached to his small body.

"Why didn't you tell me he was this bad?" Dan senior asked.

"I didn't want to worry you, dad."

"Worry me? It's not as if I have a lot to do these days."

"I'm sorry, dad. It was so sudden: one minute he was running in the garden, the next, he was in here." He wasn't going to tell his father what had made Daniel run into the garden and crack his skull on the flagstone path. Even now Jeff was sick at the thought of it.

"You were in this very same hospital to have your appendix out. Do you remember, lad?"

"It's not something I'm going to forget, dad. I almost died."

"There was never any question of that," the old man said. "Your mum was worried sick, but they got you right in a few days."

Jeff was about to say that, no, if he hadn't got to hospital, he'd have died, and it was no thanks to him if he'd survived, when Caroline walked into the room, clutching her coat, knitting basket, fresh flowers and several books and magazine. Her surprise at seeing them in the room made her drop everything. Jeff bent down and to help.

She rallied and said, "How are you, Dad?"

"Fine," he answered. "But how is Daniel? Will he be alright?"

Caroline explained the doctor's prognosis, with Jeff chipping in from time to time.

"Would you like a cup of tea, dad?" Jeff asked. "In the café. What about you Caroline?"

"No thanks. I haven't got long today. I'll stay with Daniel."

The two men walked along the corridors that smelled faintly of antiseptic in search of the hospital café.

"What were you about to say when Caroline came in?" Dan asked.

Jeff was embarrassed by the resentment that he felt because his father seemed to be showing much more concern for Daniel than he had ever shown for him. "It was nothing, dad."

"You probably thought I didn't care that you were ill," Dan senior began.

"Oh, no, dad, it wasn't...." Jeff said, his embarrassment mounting. But it was true, wasn't it? That's exactly what he'd thought.

"Let me finish," Dan senior said. "Your mother used to complain that I never showed you any affection. But that was how it was in them days. Fathers were strict and mothers were soft. That's how my father treated me, and how his father treated him." The two men walked on in silence to the café. Jeff was shocked. That was probably the longest and most meaningful conversation that he'd ever had with his father since his mother's passing. Perhaps his mother had been right when she'd said Dan senior cared for him in his own way but didn't know how to show it. "He doesn't have the words," she'd say, apologising for her husband.

* * *

The broad street leads Daniel and Eireis to an open space in front of a main gate, which is a miniature fortress in its own right with four turrets and battlements that are higher than the surrounding walls. The massive doors to the outside world are shut and barred and protected by a portcullis and a drawbridge over a broad moat, now clear of debris and full of dark, brackish water. A company of warriors marches up to relieve the guards at the gate. Daniel and Eireis look on as the warriors in their military finery, their long green capes, round shields, and spears with barbs on the end of shafts twice as tall as the warriors, form into two lines.

"Come," Eireis says, "Let's go up to the walls. We can see the whole Green Kingdom from there."

The two warriors guarding the stairway that leads to the walkway on top of the city walls step aside as Eireis and Daniel approach. They bow stiffly to the Caller of the Argaë but look at her companion – the stranger – with suspicion. But all the Argaë know that the stranger is now under the Archon's personal protection. They climb the staircase that leads to the top of the wall. At intervals, a landing gives access to rooms built within the walls. They are full of stones, vats of oil, arrows and spears – everything needed to defend the Citadel walls from an assault. Finally, they reach the top of the staircase that opens out onto a wide walkway. Warriors stand guard at intervals looking out over the plain, but they're spaced far enough apart for Daniel and Eireis to speak privately.

Daniel gazes in wonder at the broad expanse of the plain that he'd seen briefly from the window of his room in the Archon's Tower. It's only now that he can fully appreciate the kingdom's size and diversity.

"There are many tribes living in the Green Kingdom," Eireis explains. "There are the Urtikai," she says, pointing to a series of encampments surrounded by high wooden palisades that in some places are only a few paces away from the moat of the Citadel. "You saw them in the cavern," she says. Daniel remembers the fierce warriors clad in yellow-and-blue as they burst into the crystal cavern. "They are our closest neighbours, and thus both our greatest friends and our greatest foes."

"Friends!" Daniel exclaims. "They would have killed you all."

"It is a bit more complicated than, stranger," she replies, "We fight, of course, but at other times we cooperate. It is all a matter of balance. Look over there," she says pointing at another area of the plain.

The Urtikai are just one of the many dozens of tribes Daniel can see living on the plain. Eireis names them and describes their homes: the Chardri, who live atop tall square towers bristling with spiky defences; the Altii, builders of fortified village; the Rufal, who dwell in houses built on stilts or floating pontoons on rivers and lakes; the Sumira, the Cloer and far too many others for Daniel to remember. He studies in turn single buildings, encampments, villages, walled towns and strongholds of every design, and on the rare open spaces, the flimsy tents of the nomadic tribes with no permanent homes. On the horizon stand great looming shapes that Daniel thinks are mountains that ring the kingdom.

Eireis follows his gaze to the horizon. "Those are the fortresses of the Great Kings," she says. "They are the most terrible creatures and the mightiest beings in the Green Kingdom. Where they dwell, no other tribes may find water to drink nor sun to warm themselves, so says the lore of the Argaë. Yet, they stand guard over the kingdom, and without them we could not survive."

"You spoke of the Urtikai as both your enemies and friends. How can they be both?" he asks.

"Is it not so in your own world?" she asks. "The many tribes fight one another, it is true, but they also recognise that if one vanquished all the others, the balance of the kingdom would be upset, and none would survive. Even the Great Kings, who could crush us all, know this. For one to survive, all must survive."

Daniel once again probes his mind. "We, too, have wars," he says, grasping at whisps of memory. "But I'm not sure we've learned that lesson yet."

The two fall silent for a while.

Daniel, seeking a distraction from his own thoughts, scans the plain once more. He spots a small run-down village, built not far from the city walls, just beyond a much larger Urtikai encampment, whose palisade has been built across the village's main street and through several of its houses. "What tribe are they?" he asks.

The surviving houses seem to be constructed in several styles at once, so that, in one case, the lower floor is a round stone tower, the middle floor is square and of half-timbered construction, and the upper floor and roof are gabled, with bright green tiles and golden roof ornaments in the shape of animals. No two of the houses, nor any two of their floors, are alike. Looking more closely, Daniel sees that the houses are on the verge of collapse. But the villagers have more troubles. It's not just the Urtikai who have encroached on their land – other tribes have settled in the middle of the village's main street and in the gardens of the houses.

"They are a poor, wretched tribe," Eireis says. "In the past, many parts of the Green Kingdom were theirs. They were many, strong and vigorous." But instead of explaining further, she says, "Now that we're alone, tell me what you know about the time of ice and darkness that we call Whiteday."

The Pool of Life

"Hello, I'm home," Jeff said as he opened the front door.

Caroline was in the kitchen making dinner. "I'm in here," she replied. She was wiping her eyes, hoping he wouldn't notice that she'd been crying. It was so silly – she'd been making mash potatoes because they were one of Daniel's favourites, and she'd thought of him covering the mash in a spiral of ketchup before mixing into a disgusting pink mess. Then it had struck her: Daniel would not be coming home to eat dinner – he might never come home again. She'd burst into tears, and she was sure she looked a mess. It was easy for Jeff, she thought, he was a man. Everything was easier for men. They were always in control of their lives and the world.

Jeff came in and stood behind her. He put his hands hesitantly on her shoulders. In recent years, it had become an unaccustomed act of intimacy between them, and they both stood frozen for a moment: he not daring to go further, and her not knowing what to make of this sign of tenderness. She pressed into him, and he put him arms around her. The tears welled in her eyes, and she started to cry again. She turned and pressed her face into the shoulder of his suit. It smelled of what she thought as his orderly man's world of office and car.

"It'll be alright," he said. But, inside, he was as desolate as she was.

* * *

"You talked of the ice and darkness, but how can you know the secrets that only the loremasters know?" Eireis asks.

"You're not a loremaster but it seems that you know as well," he replies.

"That is true, but I am also Caller of the Archon's Tower, and I have duties that give me access to the lore and much other secret knowledge of the Argaë." She reveals no more about her duties but questions him further. To the best of his recollection, Daniel tells her of his awakening on the plain and of his wanderings through the wastes of wind and ice until he'd reached the ruins of the Citadel.

"And you say you saw and heard the Lethe?" she asks overawed. He describes the icy mist, recalling how it had pursued him into the ruined Citadel. "I have only read about the Lethe in the archives of the Tower of the Lore. None in the Green Kingdom – not even the Great Kings – have seen what you have seen or walked when you have walked. Truly, you are from another place far beyond this kingdom. No wonder Margrave is afraid of you. He fears that you have powers that are much beyond his own. He will not rest until you are banished or dead."

Daniel does not feel that he has any special powers. He seems to have spent most of his time in the Green Kingdom cold, alone, miserable, in fear of his life or unconscious. "Maybe I should leave the Citadel."

Eireis shrugs her shoulders dismissively. "And where would you go? Out there?" she asks indicating the plain with a wide sweep of her hand. "Even as we speak, warriors are on the march all over the kingdom. You have no people to defend you but the Argaë, no place of safety but the Citadel." Daniel hangs his head in despair. "But do not fear. I'll stand by you. I'll find a way of getting you back home. We are an ancient people, and our archives stretch back to the very beginning of the Green Kingdom." She turns towards the Citadel and the squat bulk of the Tower of the Lore.

"But you said that the loremasters were my enemies. Why would they help me?"

"They want you gone. That's reason enough for them."

"And if they won't help me?"

"Then we'll find another way to solve the mystery of your origin and why you were sent here. I have other sources of knowledge that I alone can call upon," she says mysteriously. "Come, let's go back to the Archon's Tower."

When they emerge from the doorway leading from the wall stairs, they see a column of several hundred warriors making ready to leave the Citadel. In addition to their spears and shields, the soldiers carry ladders, ropes and grappling irons, and behind them, on carts drawn by draft animals, are siege engines, battering rams and catapults.

Daniel stops transfixed. "I've seen all this before," he says suddenly.

"Where?" Eireis asks.

"I don't know," he answers. "For a second, I could swear that I had seen all this before," he says indicating the warriors waiting to go into battle. "But not like this – like the pictures on the walls of the Archon's Tower, only moving...." His voice trails away. The image has gone from his mind as quickly as it had come."Pictures that move?" she says, trying to imagine something so fantastic. "How is such a thing possible?"

* * *

The Greenacres garden was bursting into life. The grass, dormant throughout the winter, was sending forth new shoots, as were the weeds. Nettles and thistles crowded out the few cultivated plants left in the flowerbeds and encroached on the lawn. Caroline had hacked ineffectually at the worst of the invaders, cutting their stalks but leaving the roots untouched, ensuring that they'd grow back even more vigorously.

In the back garden, beyond the ivy-covered archway, the briar was in full spring growth. The established canes were covered in fresh green leaves, and new canes were pushing upwards and outwards through the old woody growth, while suckers were colonising any unoccupied ground they could find. Wherever the briar had yet to expand, less vigorous plants fought to establish themselves, turning the garden into a battlefield, with land gained and lost between different species.

* * *

Daniel follows Eireis to the Archon's Tower, still trying to make sense of the brief flash of memory he'd experienced when he'd seen the warriors waiting at the gate. As they walk back through the Citadel, he sees that all the towers are now topped with mirrors. All around him, water is surging upwards in the towers, reaching their summit, where it interacts with the sunlight to create both the food and power that the Argaë need to live and build. Now, the Citadel is full of new forms of activity. Carts loaded with round pods of different colours, each as big as his head are being unloaded and carried into the towers. They're followed by catapults that are hauled up by ropes to the top of the towers, where they are set up around the mirrors.

The Argaë are so engrossed by these new tasks that Eireis feels able to whisper a quick explanation to Daniel, "The artificers are making ready for the Ceremony of the Calling." Then in her normal voice, she adds, "I must prepare myself for the ceremony as well. But Chirrip will keep you company." The little creature has come out of the Archon's Tower to meet them. It shrieks excitedly and jumps onto Daniel's shoulder. "Take care not to stray and be watchful of your words." She shows him a sundial on a low pedestal in front of the tower, "When the sun enters the second quadrant," she says, indicating the second line on the face of the sundial, "it will be time for the Calling of the Unseen Ones. Come back to the Archon's Tower then."

He bids her goodbye and walks away from the tower. He wishes he could find somewhere quiet where he can think about the things he's seen, but the Citadel doesn't have any empty space. He could try to go back to the walls, but he doubts whether the soldiers would allow him onto the battlements without Eireis. He wonders aimlessly, trying to keep out of the way. Chirrip, too, is quiet, though only because he has found something to eat. he chews slowly and contentedly on some kind of fruit, perched on Daniel's shoulder. Daniel stops to look at one of the many sundials that are scattered throughout the Citadel. The first quadrant is almost over. He turns away and finds himself at the back of the squat, dark Tower of the Lore.

Here, too, preparations are underway for the Calling. The door is open, and heavily laden Argaë porters file in under the watchful eyes of a loremaster at a low doorway.

This is my chance, he thinks. I can sneak into the tower and look for the ancient records that Eireis had talked about. He puts Chirrip down. "Go back to the Archon's Tower," he orders the small creature. Chirrip hesitates but then scurries off.

As a sign of respect, the Argaë bringing supplies into the tower have covered their head with their cowls. Daniel pulls his over his head to hide his face and eyes. He goes to the end of the file and picks up a blue pod. Despite its size, it's surprisingly light. Expecting it to be heavy, he fumbles with it and almost drops it.

"Less speed, friend," the Argaë behind him says in a hushed voice. "Remember, they are the future of the Argaë."

Daniel nods, keeping his head bowed, lest his eyes give him away. He carries the pod into the tower. He holds his breath as he passes through the low doorway, but the loremaster barely spares him a second glance.

As soon as he's inside, Daniel begins to regret his hasty decision. The Argaë porters know exactly where they have to deliver their loads. He doesn't dare raise his head and look around because he's afraid that his eyes will give him away. The Argaë in front of him turns to the right. He follows, hoping that it's the right direction.

"Hey, you!" a voice says. A loremaster steps in front of him, blocking his path. "That is a blue a-nitri ball you carry, why are you taking it to the red Lar-i-nat launcher? What would the Unseen Ones say if they received a-nitri mixed with Lar-i-nat?" The thought makes him laugh. He grabs Daniel by the shoulders and turns him around until he is facing another line of retreating Argaë. Without a word, he sets off after them. "The youth of today..." the loremaster mutters to himself.

That was a close one, Daniel thinks. Then he realises that there is no one behind him; he's the last in the line of porters that has started to climb a spiral stair that leads upwards towards the top of the tower. He looks around. No one is watching. Instead of following the others, he climbs a few steps down the spiral stair until he's sure he's out of sight. The staircase is poorly lit, and he pulls off his cowl to see more clearly. He hides the a-nitri ball in an alcove and starts to climb downwards. He's sure that what he seeks will be in the caverns beneath the tower and not above.

The first landing he comes to opens out into a circular hall. With all the commotion above, the lower parts of the tower are deserted. The walls are covered in painted carvings, but even a cursory examination tells him that they're the familiar scenes of the Archon and his attendants and of the Argaë carrying out their yearly tasks that he's seen many times all over the Citadel. He continues his descent. There are no more landings or doorways, only stairs going down deeper into the earth. After several dozen steps down, there are no more torches to light his way. He climbs back and takes the last torch from its wall bracket. He counts the steps. After two hundred, he guesses that he's gone deeper than the crystal cavern under the Archon's Tower.

The staircase ends, and he emerges into a low, narrow tunnel carved out of the living rock. Here, too, the walls are covered with painted carvings. They depict the Argaë, or a tribe that resembles them, as well as pictures of dozens of other tribes he's seen on the plain. The tunnel continues, and the pictures on the walls change to gruesome scenes of carnage, as Argaë and other tribes of the Green Kingdom are being attacked by huge, terrifying monsters. One, all bloody fangs and claws, tramples over the dismembered bodies of dead Argaë, a necklace of their severed heads around its neck; another is a nightmare of tentacles, each tipped with a curved claw – all the monsters, he notes, are shown with blue or red eyes – no wonder Margrave is afraid of him. He must think I'm one of them.

In the next panel, the monsters are show fighting among themselves, and against the Argaë and the other tribes of the plain. The next shows a quite different scene: beautiful creatures with giant wings fly over the Citadel and scatter what look like snowflakes over the Argaë, who lift up their arms in welcome.

At last, the tunnel opens into a small rock chamber, which is bare of all ornament or furnishings. All it contains is circular pool of water. This place appears to be even more ancient than the tunnels that lead to it. Daniel notices indentations in the stone floor left by the footprints of other visitors made over what must be an incalculable passage of time. After checking the chamber for other entrances and finding none, he returns to the pool.

It is irregular in shape and quite unremarkable when compared to the one in the cavern under the Archon's Tower, which is perfectly round, with a finely carved rim. The water is clean and clear but so deep that it appears black. As he watches, a bubble breaks the surface, then another. In a few moments, the water is churning like a boiling caldron. He steps back in alarm. A column of water rises from the pool and takes shape as he watches. It sprouts a head, arms and legs, but four too many arms for any tribe of the kingdom he's yet to see.

The watery figure peers at him through transparent eyes. "You may ask four questions of me. What is it that you seek?" the watery figure asks.

At first, Daniel is too surprised to speak. Finally, he manages to say, "What are you?"

"I am a tear in the Ocean of Life. I am the Soul of the Argaë born at the beginning of the Second Coming," it answers mysteriously. "You have asked your first question, now ask your second question." As it speaks, it changes shape, sprouting an extra head and losing a pair of arms and legs.

"Hey, that's not fair," Daniel complains.

"Fair?" What is fair?" the Soul of the Argaë asks.

Oh, so it's like that, is it. What should I ask? What is it that I really need to know? Daniel thinks. "Who am I?" he asks.

It studies him and answers, "You are not of the First Coming, when life had yet to have shape or order, when it was divided and incomplete; nor are you of the Second Coming, when the Argaë were born into the Green Kingdom. You are not of any tribe of the Green Kingdom, you are of the Third Coming, born in the Red Kingdom."

Mystified by this reply, Daniel tries another tack: "How did I get here?"

"You are here because the Soul of the World bade the Unseen Ones to build a bridge between the kingdoms," the Soul of the Argaë replies.

The Soul of the World. Who had told him that name? "What is the Soul of the World?"

"The Soul of the World is the sum total of all life in the two kingdoms. She is the soul of all, both green and red. Your tribe has forgotten the Soul of the World, but you must make them remember, otherwise all will perish," the Soul of the Argaë replies.

The column of water loses cohesion and begins to dissolve into the pool.

"No wait!" Daniel calls out. "Tell me how I can go home! Please! Wait!" But he's had his four questions. Within seconds the pool is as black and still as it was when he'd first entered the cavern. Thinking over the replies that he's received, Daniel begins to retrace his steps back up to the surface.

* * *

"I've never seen a case like it," the registrar tells the consultant. "The patient appears comatose and unresponsive, but during the scans his hippocampus and frontal cortex were lit up like Christmas trees."

The consultant opens one of Daniel's eyes and shines a light into it. The pupil contracts at it adjusts to the sudden brightness.

"Do you think he might be a suitable candidate?" the registrar asks.

"I'd say he'd be ideal," the consultant replies. "Do you think his parents would give their consent?" he asks.

The doctor thinks for a moment and says, "Knowing them, I think they'd try anything to get him back."

* * *

Daniel has climbed back to ground level. All is quiet in the entrance hall of the Tower of the Lore. The porters and loremasters are all gone, and the low entrance door is shut and bolted. Staying close to the wall, he inches silently towards the entrance.
"I knew you would come, stranger," Margrave steps out of the shadows and blocks Daniel's path to the door. Daniel wheels round but several loremasters block all the exits from the hall except one. It must be a trap, he thinks, but what else can he do? He darts through the unguarded doorway. A few steps lead into a featureless room with a single triangular window but no other doorway.

Margrave follows him in. "Do you think we leave our secrets open for all to see?" he asks. "You must be a spy, an enemy searching out our weaknesses. But whatever you found out, you'll not be able to tell our enemies. Now you shall die." He steps forward staff held in front of him like a lance. The head of the staff burst into an eerie, pale blue flame, with which he drives Daniel towards the window. "I will send you where you belong, stranger: into the Underworld!"

Margrave uses the staff to force Daniel to climb out onto the window ledge. Daniel looks for an escape route, but there are no handholds he can use to climb up or down to safety. The world outside is murky and grey. He is directly under the Citadel's main suspended street, which is supported by an intricate lattice of struts and beams that are fixed into the walls of the surrounding towers. His only chance of escape would be to reach one of the struts, but the closest is too far away to reach from an unsteady standing jump.

Margrave lunges forwards and strikes Daniel's chest with his staff. The blue fire feels icy cold. It sends an electric shock through Daniel's body. He begins to fall backwards off the ledge.

Relax, stranger, he hears a voice say in his head. *You are in my hands now.*

He falls, plummeting towards the ground. "Any time now would be good!" he screams as the ground rushes up to meet him. A shimmering pocket of air forms around him. With only a few inches to spare, his body jerks to a halt and hangs in mid-air. After a split second, gravity reasserts itself, and he drops lightly to the ground.

Cast into the Underworld

"Are you alright?" a voice asks.

Daniel opens his eyes and sees a worried face bending over him. For a moment, he doesn't know where he is. Distorted images and sensations surge through his mind. "Mum?" he says hazily. Then the memory of what took place in the Tower of the Lore comes back to him.

"I saw you fall. Are you hurt?" A boy of about his own age is standing over him. He has green-on-green eyes like Argaë, but they are a darker green with flecks of white, and while the Argaë have dark hair, his hair is so fair that it's almost white. He's dressed in a plain tunic with an embroidered collar, which may have once been white, but is now so dirty, frayed and patched that it is grey. He carries a bundle of three of four twigs tightly to his chest, as if he's afraid that Daniel will try to take them from him. Daniel sees that the boy's face and limbs are painfully thin.

Daniel sits up and pats his limbs and torso. He seems to be uninjured. "I'm alright," he says with some surprise and not a little relief. He looks up and sees the suspended street far above. I fell from a window just below the street, he realises. And I'm not hurt. Not even a scratch! Thanks, he says to his invisible saviour. The world he has been cast into is very different from the bright, clean, sunlit world of the Citadel. Little light descends from the surface, and the air feels chilly and damp. Moisture condenses on the lower storeys of the towers. Makeshift containers – discarded Argaë pots and buckets – are laid out around the bases of the towers to collect water.

So, this is the Underworld, he thinks. What he saw when he first entered the ruined Citadel begins to make sense to him. He is amidst the piles of debris that he had clambered over, which are now far below the level of the new walkways.

"Who are you?" Daniel asks the boy.

"I am Edrelan of the Cloer Tribe," he replies.

The Cloer – Daniel recalls the name when Eireis had shown him the plain from the Citadel's battlements. He tries to remember what manner of tribe they are. Eireis had pointed out their fortified roundhouses, whose windows and doors open inward onto a central courtyard. The thick walls are no more than three or four floors high, with the rooves sloping inwards, leaving a large circular courtyard open to the sky.

A beam of sunlight that somehow manages to penetrate into the Underworld through a temporary opening high above catches Daniel's blue eyes. "You have sky-tinted eyes!' the boy cries out excitedly. "Shal-indri has come. You've come to save us!" He tugs at Daniel's clothes, urging him to follow him. "We must go to the elder."

"No," Daniel says. "You don't understand. I'm just a stranger here."

But the boy is too excited to hear him. He half leads and half drags him along a narrow path cleared through the debris around the towers. The Cloer village is close by. There wasn't enough space for them to build a full-sized roundhouse like the ones he saw on the plain, but they've done their best, incorporating the bases of the Argaë towers into their walls. The roof of roundhouse is pitted with holes and much repaired. Daniel understands with horror that the Argaë still cast whatever they no longer need nor want into the Underworld.

"Shal-indri! Shal-indri has come to set us free!" the boy calls out.

Men, women and children stop their work and come out of the roundhouse to greet the newcomers. They, too, are dressed in rags and painfully thin; many show scars and injuries from the falling debris cast down from above. They look like ghosts, Daniel thinks. But at the word "Shal-indri", a sudden hope fills their eyes, and they smile and cheer. The crowd makes way for the village elder, an old man dressed in a patched cloak who drags a crushed leg and walks with the help of a staff. He looks into Daniel's eyes. "How long we have waited for your coming," he says, bowing as deeply as an injured leg will allow him.

The crowd falls silent, waiting for Daniel's words. "I'm sorry," he says. "I'm not anyone special. I'm just a stranger...." His voice trails off as he sees the smiles vanish from the faces of the Cloer, and the light of hope die in their eyes. Slowly, they turn and return to their tasks, leaving only Edrelan and the elder in the courtyard.

"But your eyes..." Edrelan says.

The elder puts him arm around Edrelan to comfort him and says sadly, "Come by the fire, stranger."

He leads Daniel to a round hearth on which a meagre fire made up of a few twigs is almost burned out. He invites Daniel to sit and takes his own place opposite him. Edrelan respectfully deposits his bundle of twigs in front of the elder, who picks one to add to the fire. The glow as it catches alight dispels the gloom for a moment.

"Tell me your story, stranger," the elder asks Daniel.

Daniel recounts his adventures from his arrival in the Green Kingdom until his fall into the Underworld. The old man listens, and at each new revelation from his guest, he exclaims, "Such a wonder!" and "But how can this be?"

When Daniel has finished, the elder says, "And you were cast down into the Underworld and yet suffered no injury."

Daniel nods and says, "Yes, I'm not sur I understand why."

"Maybe Edrelan's words hold more truth than even you know, stranger," the elder says. "If you had not come from the sky, the Argaë would not have welcomed you, and you would not have survived such a great fall."

Daniel stares into the fire as the elder speaks, seeking clues as to his origins and identity. He focuses on the flames, trying to block out his surroundings. The answer he's searching for are just out of reach in some recess of his memory. In his mind's eye, the flame expands and changes colour. He's staring at a screen of moving pictures. It's happening again, just like when he saw the warriors lined up in front of the main gate of the Citadel. Only this time, the visions he sees are unlike anything he knows in the Green Kingdom: men, women and children led away at gunpoint by men in uniform; soldiers marching; tanks and armoured vehicles advancing through ruined streets; bombs falling from aircraft.

He senses the presence of two people behind him. But try as he might, he cannot turn his head to look at them. They're talking about the pictures on the screen.

"It's such a shame! Someone should do something about it," a woman's voice says. He is sure he's heard the voice before, but he can't remember where or when.

"Should have bombed the lot of them," a man's voice says harshly. It, too, is so maddingly familiar. Are these voices from my past?

"As if violence has ever solved anything," the woman's voice counters angrily.

The two voices continue to argue, and Daniel turns his attention back to the screen. It, too, is talking, though he can only make out a few words: "war", "refugees", "peace talks" and "ethnic cleansing". Is this the world I come from? he asks himself sadly.

A hand touches his shoulder. "Are you alright, stranger?" Edrelan asks.

Daniel is brought back to the dismal gloom of the Underworld. "I'm sorry. I was trying to remember something," Daniel explains. "But please tell me your story. How is it that you are here?"

"Once, many generations ago," the elder begins, "all this land belonged to the Cloer. Here we dwelt with our neighbours, the Chadri, the Urtikai and many other tribes of the plain. We sometimes fought with them, but there was enough land, light and water for all, and for the most part, we lived in harmony. Our villages were finely built and many, our people happy and healthy." He pauses and stares into the fire. "But then the first Argaë came," he says bitterly. "They built their first tower here, not far from this village. It was small, and we did not think it was a threat. We did not know of the Argaë then; we smiled at their efforts, like parents smile at the efforts of a child. Had we but understood what was to come.... During the following Greenday, there was not one tower, but ten. They built their walls and dug their moat, and by then we knew it was too late. Within a few generations, there were a hundred towers, and most of the Cloer villages had disappeared. We are the only one left, surviving as best we can on what the Argaë discard."

"But why do you stay?" Daniel asks.

"We are trapped here, stranger," the elder replies with a sigh. "If we tried to climb up, the Argaë would kill us. Most of us will die here, but we have one last hope for our children." He stands up stiffly. Edrelan offers him his arm, but he elder refuses it. "Come, stranger, I have something to show you." Daniel follows him to what would be the centre of the village if it were whole and round. The old man stops in front of a circular pool, which is almost dry. Only a little brackish water stands in the bottom. An obelisk made of polished black stone, about twice as tall as the elder, stands in the centre of the pool.

"This is our most treasured possession and our last hope," he says with pride tinged with sadness. He raises his hands and chants words in a language that Daniel does not understand. The only word that he recognises is "Shal-indri," which the elder repeats several times. The obelisk, as if obeying his commands, begins to rotate slowly. The tip opens, and a golden light fills the village. As the obelisk picks up speed, its black sides fall away, revealing a golden spire within.

"It's beautiful," Daniel says.

The elder lowers his arms, as if exhausted by the effort and the spire slows and closes again. "But what good is it down here? How will the Shal-indri ever find it?"

"Who are the Shal-indri?" Daniel asks.

"The Shal-indri are the People of the Sky. The Argaë call them the Unseen Ones," the elder explains.

"If but one of them can come down to us during the time of the Calling, something of us can be saved."

"The time of the Calling must be soon," Daniel says, remembering Eireis's words. "Will you show me a way back to the Citadel? I promise I'll do all I can to help you."

The elder turns to Edrelan. "Show him the way up to the Citadel. Maybe the stranger will be able to help us somehow."

"I have been to the surface many times," Edrelan says. "When I was stronger, I could travel under the streets and steal food from the Argaë as they passed by in their carts. "They never managed to catch me although they chased me many times," he adds proudly.

The two leave the village and make for the base of a nearby Argaë tower. Daniel looks up at the street many storeys above his head. A pile of debris has been shored up to give access to a window two floors above ground level.

"I had to tunnel through the debris that filled the outer room, but the corridor and staircase beyond are mostly clear," Edrelan explains. "There is no light, but you will find your way if you follow the rope that I tied to guide myself when I first went up to the Citadel. It will lead you to another window just beneath the street."

Daniel shakes Edrelan by the hand and says, "I shan't forget you."

"Shal-indri be with you, stranger."

Return from the Underworld

Daniel's journey back up to the Citadel is arduous but uneventful. Edrelan watches as Daniel disappears through the window. He looks out again and signals to Edrelan that he's found the rope to guide himself through the unlit interior of the tower. Daniel wonders how Edrelan managed to tunnel through the rubble that filled the room to reach the corridor, and from there, cleared the way to the staircase. As soon as he enters the tower, Daniel can hear the powerful surge of water that shoots up the central well from the underground cavern. They take most of the water and light, he thinks sadly, leaving almost nothing for the Cloer.

He can see little of the interior, but the rope is a sure guide, and Daniel makes good time as he travels upwards in the abandoned section of the tower. Long ago, these rooms were new and echoed with life. Was Eireis ever in here? he wonders. The Argaë are not bad people, he thinks as he climbs. They work hard and do their best according to their customs and lore. And they have been kind to him, a stranger – well, most of them have been kind to him. On the other hand, they've stolen the Cloer's land and starved them of light and water and access to the Shal-indri, the Unseen Ones. He does not know what he can do, but he is determined to help the Cloer if he can. Maybe Eireis will know of a way.

After climbing in darkness, the rope leads him to a narrow passage through another outer room cleared by Edrelan. He looks out of the window and sees that he is directly under the citadel's broadest suspended street. He can hear the thundering of hundreds of feet and cartwheels on the planking and the voices of Argaë as they pass overhead. The whole intricate structure of struts and supports driven into the sides of the surrounding towers vibrates and shudders alarmingly. Yet when he walked along the broad avenue, it felt as firm as solid ground.

The final leg of the climb out of the underworld – the jump from a window to the nearest strut of the Citadel's main street, is also the riskiest. He knows that he has fallen from the same height without hurting himself, but he's not willing to repeat the experience to test his invulnerability. The gap is no more than three of four feet, but at this height, it might as well be a mile across. He looks down and sees Edrelan's upturned face far below.

"*Cry baby!*" a man's voice echoes in his head. He can make out the annoyed tone, the contempt, but he still can't remember who the man is.

A woman's voice joins the first. He knows it too. "*Daniel, don't! You'll hurt yourself,*" she says in a pleading tone.

Yes! Daniel! Daniel is my name, he says aloud. He's overjoyed because he's finally managed to remember something concrete about himself and his past. He's afraid of the jump, but he must do it. He can't stay on this window ledge forever. He looks down once more. The tiny figure of Edrelan is waving at him in encouragement. He counts, "One, two, three!" and jumps.

* * *

"What time will you be back?" Caroline asked. She was smiling to herself.

"About seven. I have a meeting in town. I'll have to drive back in the rush hour. Don't expect me to be in a good mood after an hour stuck in traffic," Jeff replied, but any trace of annoyance had gone from his voice. "This bread is good. I'll have another piece, please. Are you going to the hospital today?" he asked.

"Yes... I'll look in this morning after I've done the shopping," she replied. She hadn't been going to see Daniel as often lately. The doctor had told her that he could come around at any moment, but there had been no change for several weeks. She told herself she must go visit him today.

She had to go to see her own doctor in any case, and his surgery was on the way to the hospital.

"What have you got to be so happy about?" Jeff asked.

"Oh, I'm just in a good mood I suppose – it's such a nice day," she said, but she had another, and as yet unconfirmed reason to be happy. But she wasn't going to tell him until she knew for sure.

"I'll see you later, darling." He kissed her and left.

She listened to the car drive off and looked out onto the sunlit garden. Jeff had tidied up the flowerbeds in the front garden, and re-seeded the lawn where it was patchy after years of neglect, but the rear garden, hidden beyond the ivy-covered fence was just the same as the day they'd moved in.

It was a big job, and they didn't have the time – especially with Daniel in hospital.

A spot of gardening would do her good, she decided. She picked up her gardening gloves and the secateurs from the kitchen sideboard and walked out into the garden. There were weeds everywhere. They had sprung back in the flowerbeds and the lawn. The ivy had grown too, closing off the archway into the back garden once more. She cut the suckers away until she had created an opening wide enough to look through.

The canes were covered in bright green leaves and showed the tiny buds that would ripen into plump purplish-black fruit.

"Well, at least I'll be able to make blackberry jam this year," she said to herself. "If I can ever get in there to pick them."

* * *

Daniel has overestimated the distance and hits the strut hard. He bounces off but just managed to catch hold of a neighbouring strut with his outstretched hands. He's hanging over the sheer drop, his arms aching from the strain of holding his full weight. He kicks with his legs and manages to wrap them around a neighbouring strut. His legs secure, he pulls himself over the top of a horizontal beam. From there it is a relatively easy climb along a joist that leads to a hatch that opens onto the suspended street. He'd seen the Argaë use them in the past, to dump their rubbish, not realising then that the Citadel's castoffs dropped liked bombs onto the Cloer village below.

An Argaë calls out in alarm as Daniel heaves himself up onto the street. The traffic stops, and the Argaë gather around him.

"It's the stranger come back to us!" one Argaë says excitedly.

While they do not sound exactly delighted to see him again, nor are they angry or threatening.

A patrol of warriors, attracted by the disturbance in the orderly routine, arrives on the scene.

"The Lord Keeper told the Council that you had returned to the Sky to prepare for the Calling," a puzzled Argaë warrior tells Daniel.

"Clear the way! Clear the way and go about your business," the officer in charge of the patrol orders. He, too, seems surprised to see Daniel. "Stranger, you have returned. The Caller ordered that we search high and low for you in the Citadel but no trace of you could be found."

Whatever story Margrave had concocted to explain his sudden disappearance, he had not revealed Daniel's visit to the Tower of the Lore.

"I came back because I wished to see the Calling for myself," Daniel explains, trying to sound as assured as possible. "Now, take me to the Caller."

Eireis is overjoyed. "Stranger! I thought you had left us," she says as she greets him in the audience chamber of the Archon's Tower.

The chamber is empty now. The warriors are manning the walls or fighting on the plain, and the citizens are busy with the preparations for the Calling. Daniel tells her of his adventures since they parted: his entry into the Tower of the Lore, Margrave's attack, his fall into the Underworld, his meeting with the Cloer, and his climb back to the Citadel.

"The Archon shall hear of this outrage!" she says.

"That will not help me to get back," he counters. "I have a favour to ask from you." He explains about the Cloer and about their hope to reach an Unseen One.

She looks serious for a moment and moves away from him. "I cannot help them," she says.

"Why not?" he asks.

"The Cloer are our enemies. Don't you see? If the situation were different and we were in the Underworld and they above, they would behave just the same."

"But all they want to do is for their children to leave. What harm would that do to the Argaë?"

"You don't know what you ask," she says. "Is it any different in your world?"

Daniel recalls the moving pictures on the screen – the soldiers, the children crying, the houses burning. "I'm not sure," he says, struggling to remember. "Terrible things happen there, too, but I think that some of us try to be better if we can."

At this precise moment, Margrave sweeps into the room. "So, it's true," he spits out bitterly. "The stranger has returned."

"Yes, Margrave. No thanks to you," Eireis says coldly. "Now, will you believe that he is the messenger of the Unseen Ones?"

"I will keep my counsel about what I believe, Caller. But I come here as the bearer of good tidings for the stranger." He smiles but there's no joy in his smile, only spiteful triumph.

Eireis instinctively draws near to Daniel as if to shield him with her body. "What news, Margrave?" she asks.

"I have just come from the Archon who busies himself with the preparations for the Calling. As soon as the ceremony is over, as is our age-old custom, the Archon will ride forth to war with the tribes of the plain for the greater glory of the Argaë. He has agreed to take the stranger, his sworn page and liege servant, on this Greenday's campaign."

"I shan't allow it!" Eireis says sharply.

"The matter is already decided, Caller. Would you stand against the Archon's wishes?"

"I'll go," Daniel says.

"It's a trick. He'll find a way to harm you once you are outside the Citadel," she whispers but loud enough for Margrave to hear.

"This is no trick, Caller," Margrave says in his most deferential tone. "It is a chance for the stranger to repay the Argaë for their kindness, and, out on the plain, he may find a way to leave the Green Kingdom and return to his home in the Sky. Now, Caller, stranger," he says, bowing low. "If there is nothing more, I must remind you of your duties for the Calling."

"There is one thing," Daniel says. "My name is Daniel."

"Da-ni-el," Margrave repeats the name slowly as if tasting something bitter. "I shall record it in the archives of the Argaë."

Margrave bows stiffly and sweeps out. A single cannon blast reverberates over the Citadel.

"Are we under attack?" Daniel asks.

"No. It is the signal to tell the Argaë that the second quadrant is almost over. The time of the Calling is upon us. I must prepare for the ceremony. Go to your room. I shall have appropriate clothes sent to you. You'll have a seat of honour with the Archon's pages on the summit of the Archon's Tower, and you must be dressed according to your rank."

The Calling

An Argaë servant lays out Daniel's page's uniform on the bed. He notices that the Argaë are no longer in awe or afraid of him since he's been taken under the Archon's protection. Daniel slips on a shirt of silver mail over a dark green tunic, fastens the cape of long, dark-green strands with the silver clasp, and puts on the silver belt around his waist onto which are buckled a dagger and a short sword in silver scabbards incrusted with green gems. The last item on the bed is a bag woven from the finest silken strands, each barely thicker than a human hair. It looks too delicate to use, but when he tests the strands, he finds that they are both incredibly strong and can stretch many times their own length. He slings the bag over one shoulder across his chest like a bandolier.

  He walks over to the window and looks down on the Citadel. A festival atmosphere reigns in every quarter. The towers, gates, and walls are bedecked with coloured streamers and flags. The Argaë have laid down their tools for the first time since his arrival. They throng the streets in their finery. Wherever he looks, the sun glints off ornaments of gold and silver and collars, belts and headdresses studded with precious gems. He notices that many carry the same fine-stranded bags, while others shoulder woven baskets, some so big that they have to be carried by two Argaë.

There is not enough room on the summit of the towers for everyone, so many sit out on balconies, stand along the top of the city walls or on the highest walkways between the towers. All eyes are turned expectantly towards the eastern sky. Daniel hurries to join the other guests making their way to the top of the Archon's Tower.

The spiral staircases of the tower are thronged with courtiers, pages and warriors. They greet him with, "Blessings on this Day of Calling, Da-ni-el!" Laughing, they invite him to join them in their merriment. He allows himself to be swept along until they reach the top of the tower. Tiered benches have been built in a circle around the roof facing east.

The Archon and his court are already seated in the very centre of the temporary amphitheatre. Lord Keeper Margrave sits at the head of the loremasters to the left of the Archon. Daniel's place is with the warriors and pages on the Archon's right. He looks for Eireis, but she is not in her accustomed seat next to her father.

Looking over the plain, he sees that the Argaë aren't the only ones who are celebrating the Day of Calling. All the tribes of the plain have decorated their houses, castles, towers and villages with garlands, bunting, flags and streamers. They, too, wait on their own high places for the Unseen Ones. Daniel seeks out the cluster of Cloer villages in the distance beyond the Urtikai encampments. He imagines Edrelan and the elder far below in the gloom of the Underworld, gathered around their solitary golden spire. I've failed them, he thinks sadly.

A semi-circle of catapults has been set up on a platform on the eastern side of the roof, next to them are piles of coloured pods – blue, red, green, yellow, and purple – just like those he'd carried into the Tower of the Lore. The Archon's Tower is the only tower that has another yet higher platform, hanging perilously high over its eastern battlements. The platform is currently unoccupied but a balustrade around it shows that it is intended for someone to stand on.

A second cannon blast hushes the expectant crowds. Eireis appears and walks silently through the seated crowd looking neither to her left nor right. Her hair is piled high on her head is kept in place by a sparkling band of gold hung with green gems; her silver cloak shimmers in the sunlight, and changes hue as it catches the reflections of the clothes of the courtiers and warriors.

She climbs the steps to the high platform and looks out over the plain. Raising her arms, she calls out, "Blessed be this Day of Calling. I call upon the Unseen Ones to descend from their homes in the sky to receive the bounty of the Argaë."

Daniel wonders what they will be like, these Unseen Ones, he's heard so much about. Will he recognise them as his own people and get his memory back? Eireis begins to sing in a high clear voice.

Daniel cannot make out the words of her song. Rather than distinct words, it seems to be composed of sustained notes. As her voice fades, silence falls over the entire plain.

Although there is nothing to see in the clear blue sky, Daniel feels a tingling in the air that raises the hairs on the back of his neck. He's not alone, as he feels the Argaë become tense and then relax like one great body. The very fabric of the air is vibrating as it shimmers around the towers.

"They have come!" Eireis calls out. A deafening cheer rises from the Argaë in which Daniel joins in.

The Archon stands up, draws his sword, and raises it in the air. The blade catches the sun's rays and burst into flame. At his signal, the artificers stand ready to pull the levers that will fire the catapults that are already loaded with different coloured pods.

"Fire!" the Archon shouts, bringing the sword down in a golden arc.

All over the Citadel, there is a deafening crack, as hundreds of catapults fire at the same moment.

Daniel follows the flight of the pods into the sky. Before gravity has a chance to pull them towards earth, they explode into huge gold rosettes edged in cobalt blue. Wave after wave of pods is launched, creating a dazzling array of patterns and colours – ruby and emerald, Turquoise and silver, carnelian and sapphire – like fireworks in broad daylight, he thinks. He remembers standing somewhere quite different, at nighttime. He senses the familiar presence of two people behind him. But before he can explore the memory any further, he feels a sudden rush of wind on his face.

The Unseen Ones swoop down over the plain. They are invisible to his eyes and to those of the Argaë, but their shapes are outlined as they pass through the clouds of glittering colours. For an instant, Daniel can make out the blur of gigantic wings beating the air above Eireis. Unseen Ones form a semi-circle around the platform on which she stands, arms lifted in welcome. A form many times her size, its great wings creating silver, sapphire, gold and cobalt vortices around the tower, hangs in front of her and gently touches her face.

Through the flakes of brilliant colour, she turns towards the pages, and stares straight at Daniel. She beckons him with her hand. There is a murmur of amazement in the crowd. Such a thing has ever happened in the recorded history of the Argaë – a deviation in the ceremony of the Calling. Margrave stands but is too shocked to speak. Stunned, Daniel is frozen in his seat, but the other pages urge him forwards. He makes his way to the base of the platform and climbs up into the maelstrom of swirling colours. "Come, Da-ni-el. They wish to speak to you," Eireis says. He reaches her and stands by her side in an area of complete calm. He finds himself in the eye of a multicoloured hurricane.

Another great form descends, and he feels its insubstantial touch on his face and body. He abandons himself to the touch, and his mind is filled with images of the plain as it appears through the eyes of the Unseen Ones. Confused with the images of castles, camps and villages are visions of green leaves, canes and high stalks heavy with open flowers of every shape and hue.

He feels their thoughts rather than hear the voice. *You are not of this realm,* the Unseen One says directly into his mind. *You are of the Red Kingdom's Third Creation. You were brought here by the Soul of the World to make the choices that those in the Red and Green Kingdoms cannot make for themselves.*

"I think I'm beginning to understand," Daniel says. "Did I meet you when I travelled here from the Red Kingdom?" he asks.

We have met but not then, before. The one you met was the Soul of the World who brought you here.

"I have a request – a choice," Daniel says. "At the base of the tower...." He projects the image of the Cloer in their dark Underworld towards the Unseen One. It hovers momentarily and launches itself into the sky high above the Citadel, where it joins its fellows that are weaving the coloured flakes into complex geometric patterns.

"They have read your heart, Da-ni-el," Eireis says. "They have granted you your wish for the Cloer."

An immense winged shape outlined by a trail of glittering flakes spirals downwards around the Archon's Tower.

"Thank you," he says, squeezing her hand.

"Look through their eyes," she says.

In an instant, he sees the gloom of the Underworld, and the Cloer's spire spinning like some great golden Christmas decoration, sending out sprays of gold. It's at once a spire and flower. The Unseen One flies through the golden spray that turns to silver in its wake. The vision fades.

The flakes thrown up into the air by the catapults are falling back to the ground, but they have somehow grown larger and lost their brilliant hues. They have become tiny white spheres, no larger than marbles, which float down towards the Citadel. Eireis opens the net that she carries under her cloak and begins to collect the spheres with deft movements of net and hand as soon as they come into reach. Even the Archon and Margrave are doing the same. The Argaë jump and whoop for joy as they collect the small pearly white spheres.

"Help us, Da-ni-el," she says, scooping a handful of the spheres out of the air. "Hurry! Hurry! We don't have much time."

He unfurls his own net and tries to snatch a few spheres from the tower roof. They have almost no weight, and the slightest movement sends them spiralling away.

"Like this," Eireis says, showing him how to use one hand to guide the sphere towards the mouth of the net.

* * *

Jeff and Caroline were sitting in the garden in brand-new red and white deckchairs. Early June had been wet and cold – as was traditional for Wimbledon fortnight – but for July, the weather was set fair for the next two weeks. The weathermen were even predicting a drought for August and a hosepipe ban in parts of the country, but she knew what that was worth. With Daniel still in hospital and her pregnancy, there had been little time to do much to the garden. She had made Jeff spend the morning gardening, and he had, but with bad grace and constant complaints that he was too tired from a hard week at the office.

At least he'd weeded the beds nearest to the house and mown the overgrown lawn. As he dozed in his chair, Caroline cast a critical eye over his handiwork. The lawn wasn't a meadow anymore. The weeds mowed down to their roots merged with the grass to give respectable green cover, though there were bare patches that would need reseeding. He had done the best he could with the surviving roses, clearing away the choking weeds and cutting back the dead canes. They were in bloom, but the rootstock was so old that the plants seemed unable to decide what colour their blooms should be. One leggy bush that had grown to about five or six feet high before collapsing under its own weight had brought forth a strange mixture of large yellow roses and small pink ones.

Without the weeds the beds looked a bare. A trip to the garden centre for bedding plants would deal with that. She wondered if she could persuade Jeff to go that afternoon, but she didn't rate her chances. Long hours at work, visits to Daniel, and helping her prepare for the arrival of their daughter, she admitted, had left him physically exhausted.

She knew nothing about gardening. In their city-centre flat, she'd planted window boxes at random with seeds she's found at the supermarket. A technique she'd repeated at Greenacres with mixed results. Several boxes were giving a good show, others looked as if they had sprouted weeds, refusing to produce the blooms promised in the pictures on the front of the packet. Jeff was no better. It was his first garden, and he'd never shared Dan senior's love of gardening and allotments. Perhaps she would ask the old boy for his advice next time he came to Sunday lunch. That was another change in family arrangements. Jeff went to fetch his father every Sunday morning, and they would go to the pub together while she made lunch. Roast beef with all the trimmings. They were a family again. Or maybe, it was fairer to say that they'd become a family for the first time.

Jeff and Dan senior had never been close, and Jeff had moved out as soon as he'd gone to university, never to return. Although he'd visited for Christmas for his mother's sake, he'd stopped going altogether after she'd died. When his father, too, had fallen ill, Jeff had arranged for him to go into a nursing home, claiming with some justice that their city-centre flat was far too small and impractical for an invalid. Everything had changed now. Jeff had even brought up the idea that his father should move back in with them. The local authority would provide a carer to help Caroline out, especially in the first few months after the birth of their second child.

In a way, it was all thanks to Daniel. But he was the only person who wasn't able to appreciate the changes his accident had brought about. He'd missed his birthday, though she had made a point of spending the whole day with him. She'd brought him his cards, including one signed by his whole class. She'd laid out his presents on the bed and opened them one by one for him. There was a new games console, and a selection of the latest games. She'd even got Jeff to plug it into the television in the room and marvelled at how good the graphics were. The computer games she remembered from here childhood were Tetris and Pacman, but these were like entire worlds you could just step into. She wondered where her son was – even whether he was in some other world of his own creation.

The doctors said there was no change in his condition, but they'd asked her permission to give him an experimental drug from America. At first, she'd been opposed to the idea. Her son wasn't a guinea pig to be experimented on, and anything from America was automatically suspect. But the doctor had given her some articles to read on "awakenings" – people who'd been in comas for ten or twenty years who had suddenly woken up. There was too much scientific jargon for her to read more than the first few paragraphs, and she had given them to Jeff to finish.

Her inability to follow the articles annoyed her; it made her feel inadequate. But it was for her son, so she promised herself that she would make the effort to read them.

She stood up to stretch her legs and went to inspect the archway into the back garden. The ivy had grown back since she'd cut it back in the spring. Nettles and bramble canes were sticking out through the canopy of dark-green and white leaves. There was no holding back the ivy, which had encroached onto the lawn until Jeff had attacked it with the shears and the lawnmower. There was a large pile of ivy on the path, which was the only place for it until they could reach the compost heap that had been in a bin placed against the back wall.

The bramble canes were fruiting. They had lost their delicate, pale-pink flowers, which had been replaced by the small green clusters, and that had now matured and swollen into the juicy dark purple-black berries that she remembered picking as a child with her parents on Sundays on Hampstead Heath. They'd been great walkers. She recalled long summer afternoons on the Heath or in the country, coming across great drifts of brambles. Sometimes a previous picker had already flattened the canes to make it easier to reach the best of the fruit that always seemed to be just out of reach to the young Caroline, but sometimes, they'd missed a juicy cluster of berries hidden under leaves but just at the right height for her.

"We should really do something about the back garden," Jeff said. He was standing beside her.

"Yes, it would be nice if we could do something with it for Daniel when he gets home," she replied.

– 12 –

The Wheel of the Fortunate

Daniel empties the white spheres that he's collected into a basket carried by an Argaë porter. As soon as the basket is full, the porter transfers his load into large fine-meshed nets that hang on the end of ropes over the parapet of the tower roof. All over the Citadel, every single sphere, no matter how inaccessible, is hunted down and collected – even those in the moats outside are fished out with nets at the end of long poles. Daniel pauses to look out over the plain. For once, the Green Kingdom seems at peace, as all the tribes are too busy with the Calling to fight one another.

Daniel spots a sphere hidden under a recess in the stonework of the tower's battlements. He ducks down to pick it up. He is about to drop it into the carrier's basket when he looks at it again. He could swear that it is slightly larger than the ones he's collected before and slightly pinkish green in colour. He examines the other spheres in the basket more closely. He realises that they, too, have changed, swelling and taking on the same pinkish hue.

"Hurry, hurry," Eireis says, emptying her net into the basket, "there isn't much time before they change."

Daniel watches the last basketfuls of spheres is emptied into the nets hanging over the parapet. The nets are a quarter full, but the spheres, exposed to the of the sun, are quickly expanding and darkening in colour. The nets shudder and creak, swinging gently on their tethers, as the spheres now lighter than the surrounding air begin to float upwards.

At the rate they're inflating, Daniel thinks, they will quickly fill the nets completely and float up like enormous hot-air balloons. He has a vision of a sky full of giant hot-air balloons –shaped like animals, people and houses. He's very small and stands between a man and a woman, who each hold one of his hands. The vision vanishes, leaving him frustrated again. If only I could remember, he thinks. But each time I do remember something, I forget it just as quickly.

"Hurry!" Eireis says jolting him out of his reverie. "As soon as the collection is finished," she continues, her voice full of excitement, "there will be a great festival in the Citadel, Da-ni-el, with singing, dancing, feasting and games."

The Argaë make quick work of the last few uncollected spheres and watch them as they are loaded into the last unfilled nets that hang from the sides of the tower. As soon as the collection is finished, the Argaë let out a great cheer that echoes all over the Citadel.

"And now, we shall feast and dance!" Eireis says happily, leading Daniel by the hand down the staircase to the lower city.

The streets are already thronged with Argaë in high spirits. Wherever they go, they find revellers drinking, eating, dancing and playing all manner of games. Grown men and women skip and chase one another like children, and children dance like adults. Daniel and Eireis join a ring of dancers that runs faster and faster around the base of a tower. Tired and dizzy from the frenetic dance, they make their way to the main square to watch the parade of the Archon's warriors, whose, polished helmets, weapons, armour and shields glint in the Greenday sun. After the military parade, there are races and athletics contests for the younger men and women – who can run fastest, jump highest, throw furthest. All social distinctions are forgotten as the pair goes from place to place enjoying the festival events. Better still, no one looks askance at Daniel or gives him a wide berth. This may not be home, but it's the next best thing, he thinks happily.

"What's happening there?" Daniel asks, pointing at a long file of Argaë that vanishes behind the Tower of the Lore. By a common yet unspoken consent, they have avoided the area until now, because neither of them wants to risk another meeting with Margrave. "It seems to be very popular."

"Oh, it is," Eireis replies, but there is a note of sadness in her voice that is out of keeping with the general mood of the day. "Everyone plays it. It's called the Wheel of the Fortunate."

"Are there prizes?" he asks excitedly.

"Of course," she replies, "prizes and... forfeits."

But Daniel is too excited to notice the change in her mood. He pulls her into the throng of waiting Argaë. Despite the numbers lining up to take part, they don't have to wait long before they are in sight of the Wheel. Set on a platform to raise it high above the throng, the wheel is three times the height of an adult Argaë. Its face is divided in four white sections alternating with four red sections, in addition, each section contains symbols and drawings, whose meaning Daniel cannot even guess at. Mounted on a central axis the end of which is shaped like an arrow, the wheel can be spun and will stop with the arrow inside one of the red or white sections.

Daniel watches an Argaë climb the steps to the platform. He spins the wheel which stops on a red section. A great cheer goes up among the crowd. He's handed a red token.

"Has he won?" Daniel asks.

"Everyone who spins the wheel wins something," Eircis says, as she steps up to take her turn.

Daniel is so excited by the cheering crowd and so busy looking about that he does not notice what colour the wheel stops on for Eireis. "Can I have a go?" he asks.

Eireis speaks to the Argaë in charge, who invites Daniel to take his turn. The giant wheel is surprisingly light. Daniel puts all his strength into it and takes his turn.

"White! I landed on white! What do I win?"

"Good fortune, stranger," the Argaë in charge of the Wheel says, handing him a white token. Eireis pulls him away and leads him towards the next attraction. Within minutes, Daniel has forgotten all about the Wheel of the Fortunate. He even forgets to ask what colour Eireis landed on.

Many hours later, exhausted and happy, Daniel and Eireis seek out a quiet place to rest. Eireis leads them to a small square at the rear of the Archon's Tower. A fountain-sundial, one of many in the Citadel, trickles merrily in the middle of a circle of stone benches.

"I am happy to have met you, Da-ni-el," Eireis says shyly.

"And I you, Eireis," Daniel replies no less embarrassed. It's the first time since their visit to the city walls that they've had any private time together.

They sit side by side, not saying anything.

After what seem to be an eternity of silence but is probably no more than a few minutes, he turns to face her and takes her hand. "I am glad I've met you and the Argaë. I'll never forget you. Never!"

"With your leave, Caller." A shadow falls over them. They look up to see Margrave, his head bowed in a gesture of respect that they both know he cannot possibly mean. "Caller," he says, bowing even lower. "I have come to fetch the stranger. He is to join the Archon at once at the South Gate."

She is about to say something, but Daniel steps forwards and says, "I'm ready," silencing any complaint she might make on his behalf.

"He is under my protection, as well as that of the Unseen Ones, Margrave," she warns the loremaster.

"As he is under mine, Caller. With so many friends, he is sure to win a glorious victory for the Argaë," Margrave adds with an ingratiating smile.

"Win great a victory?" Daniel says.

"Yes, stranger. The Archon in his wisdom has put you in charge of the Second Corps. He will lead the main body of the army in a frontal assault on the Urtikai encampment by the Citadel's Southern Gate, while you, stranger, will lead the second corps through a secret tunnel that leads into the heart of their camp. Undercover of the Archon's attack, you will surprise the enemy and throw open the gates to admit the main body of the army."

Unable to contain herself, Eireis cries out, "But that's a suicide mission!"

"On the contrary, Caller," Margrave says. "It is a masterful plan that our forefathers have used with great success to establish the power of the Argaë all over the Green Kingdom."

"You may leave us, Margrave. I will take Da-ni-el to the Archon myself."

"With your leave, Caller, I shall wait to accompany you both to the Archon. We would not want the stranger to lose his way." He walks away but makes sure he remains within sight of the pair.

"You mustn't go," Eireis says. "Margrave has some treachery planned."

"Margrave cannot hurt me, he's tried his worst and I'm still here," he says to comfort her, but he's not so sure of himself. "Come. Let's go see your father, the Archon."

* * *

"It's just one injection," the doctor explained. "In essence it's a single dose of an extremely powerful neurotransmitter," he went on, trying to find the words that would make sense to a layperson. "Like a very strong cup of coffee. In many cases, one dose kick-starts the brain into consciousness. The Americans have had some amazing results."

"And it's absolutely safe?" Caroline asked. She was still unsure, even after having made herself read through the articles that the doctor had sent her.

"The side-effects are minimal," he assured her. "The problems are much more likely to come from the reaction of the patient when he realises how long he's been unconscious. In Daniel's case, the shock won't be so great because he hasn't been in a coma for very long."

"You don't call five months very long?" Jeff asked.

"I was speaking relatively. He's been in a coma for a short time compared to some of the long-term cases in the United States. Of course, the most important thing is for you both to be here if the treatment is successful and he wakes up. And his grandfather, as well, if that's possible," the doctor added.

"When would you want to do it?" Jeff asked.

"The timing is very much up to you. But once you've given your consent, I'd like to proceed as soon as possible."

Caroline looked at Jeff and nodded her head. "We give our consent," he said.

"I'll have the consent form drawn up for you to sign. You can collect it from the ward sister. Would you both be able to be here tomorrow morning about eleven?"

"Tomorrow?" Caroline said, startled.

Jeff thought about it. "I should be able to get the day off. We can collect Dan senior – Daniel's grandfather – early tomorrow morning."

* * *

The Archon is resplendent in his golden armour and a dark-green cape, surrounded by his generals and captains. "Welcome, Da-ni-el," he says extending his hand.

"My lord," says Daniel bowing and holding his hand to his lips in the gesture of respect with which the Argaë warriors salute to their ruler. There is a murmur of approval among the officers at his traditional gesture of fealty. Eireis has trained him well in Argaë customs.

"We leave at once!" the Archon announces. The heralds sound the call to arms, and the portcullis of the South Gate is raised and the drawbridge lowered. The warriors march out in two columns. The column to the left is much larger, and its soldiers are heavily armed and are equipped with ropes with grappling hooks, ladders, siege engines and catapults. The column to the right is no more than 200 strong. They are lightly armed, and their cloaks are a drab grey-green colour that contrasts with the golds and greens uniforms of the main force.

They do not have to go far, as the Urtikai encampment they're attacking is built close to the Citadel's southern walls. The Urtikai warriors are furiously assaulting the Argaë battlements, attempting to scale the walls with ladders and trying to demolish the towers with catapults and siege engines of their own. At times, it seems that they have made a breech, but Argaë engineers waiting on the other side of the walls always plug them close with baulks of timbers and sacks filled with soil. The Argaë soldiers rain down spears and rocks on their attackers, but the Urtikai seem immune under the long shields that they hold over their heads. The sun is directly overhead, and Daniel sweats in his armour and full-length cloak.

The columns stop, and the Archon points away from the battle. "You are to take your detachment to the rear of the encampment where my engineers have been secretly digging a tunnel," the Archon orders Daniel. "My general will lead you."

From a high point on the city walls, Eireis watches Daniel lead the small force away from the main army and move unobserved to the far side of the Urtikai encampment.

The Archon raises his sword and orders a counterattack on the Urtikai assaulting the walls. To shield Daniel as much as possible, he has ordered his men to shout, beat drums, sound horns and wave their banners. The Urtikai, seeing that their retreat is about to be cut off, abandon their assault on the Citadel and begin to fall back towards their camp.

"Charge!" the Archon orders raising his sword. The Argaë warriors launch themselves into a headlong rush after the retreating enemy. The Archon and his personal attendants are close to the centre of the fray.

Eireis turns her attention to Daniel's party. But she is not the only one who is watching his troops enter the secret tunnel that leads under the palisade into the Urtikai encampment. Margrave is on the top of a nearby tower. He stands looking out over the parapet. He gives a signal to several loremasters, and they tilt the tower's mirror towards the Urtikai encampment.

The last of Daniel's troops have vanished into the tunnel. They only have the last few metres to dig, and they will break through inside the Urtikai encampment. The enemy commander has sent all his men to the palisade to oppose the Argaë counterattack led by the Archon. They support their men outside the encampment by bombarding the approaching Argaë with missiles. The Archon's army responds with catapult fire, and the siege towers and battering rams move forwards.

Eireis sees a bright flash out of the corner of her eye. She turns to see several of Margrave's loremasters on the summit of a nearby tower, dipping the mirror so that it shines into the Urtikai encampment. He's sending some kind of signal to the enemy! She looks back towards the unfolding battle. Urtikai warriors are racing from the palisade towards the spot where a dozen Argaë warriors, including Daniel, are just emerging from a hole in the ground.

* * *

Jeff, Caroline and Dan senior watched the doctor disinfect Daniel's arm with an alcohol swab. A nurse waited next to him, holding a tray with a hypodermic and a phial of the miracle drug. The doctor filled the hypodermic and squirted a few drops from the end to make sure that no air was left inside.

* * *

Although more Argaë are emerging from the tunnel, they're too few to resist the growing circle of Urtikai warriors around them. The Argaë have made a wall with their shields to resist the enemy assaults. But the Urtikai seem less interested in their Argaë enemies than in capturing Daniel.

"Retreat! Retreat! We've been discovered!" Daniel shouts, and his order is carried to the men in the tunnel. The Argaë warriors fall back to the tunnel opening and slide down one by one.

* * *

Caroline turned away as the doctor stuck the fine hypodermic needle into Daniel's arm. He pressed the plunger and the clear liquid flowed into Daniel's body.

"The drug can take up to twenty minutes to work," he said. "I'll be monitoring his vital signs throughout." He motioned to the monitors next to the bed.

* * *

An Urtikai warrior lashes out at Daniel with a heavy club, catching the side of his helmet. Daniel reels back and falls to the ground. Seeing their chance to capture him, the Urtikai try to grab him to pull him away, but the Argaë warriors fight them back. Daniel is lifted away from danger and passed from hand to hand down into the tunnel to safety.

* * *

The alarm shrieked from the monitors. Daniel's body was going into spasm, his back arching, limbs thrashing around. Tubes and wires were wrenched off. It took the doctor, the nurse and Jeff's combined strength to hold him down.

"His blood pressure is dropping," the doctor said when he was able to take Daniel's pulse and listen to his heart with a stethoscope. "He's going into shock. Nurse, 50cc of atropine."

The nurse rushed from the room and returned a with another hypodermic.

* * *

Daniel feels as if his spirit has been violently wrenched out of his body. For a few seconds, he sees himself lying unconscious on a hospital bed, as if he were viewing the scene from the ceiling of the room. His parents and his grandfather are there, as well as a doctor and a nurse. I finally know who I am and where I come from!

Mum. . . dad… he wants to call out to explain and reassure them, but at the same time, he's in the thick of the desperate fight between the Urtikai and the Argaë.

He struggles to return to his body in his world or the Green Kingdom but fails. Exhausted by the effort, he passes out.

The Time of Going Forth

"He's stabilising," the doctor announced with relief, removing the stethoscope from Daniel's chest. "I don't understand," he went on, turning to the shocked Caroline, Jeff and Dan senior. "There's never been such a violent reaction to the drug reported in the literature."

"Your literature is obviously wrong!" Jeff growled angrily, trying to comfort Caroline who was sobbing quietly. Moments later, when they were all standing in the corridor outside Daniel's room, Jeff finally said to the doctor, "He'll come round when he's good and ready! What have I paid taxes for all these years! Not for you to experiment on him! For God's sake!"

"Darling..." Caroline said, holding onto his arm, and trying to calm her husband down.

"I'm truly sorry. We've never had such an adverse reaction. The case studies so far have—"

"I don't care about your case studies! Daniel isn't a laboratory rat. He is my son!"

"Come on, lad," Dan senior said. "They were only trying to do their best for the boy."

Still angry and shouting at the doctor, Jeff let his father and wife lead him away towards the exit.

When they were gone, the doctor went back in to check on Daniel's condition. "I've never seen anything like it," he said to the nurse who was tucking in Daniel's bedsheets. "I could swear he regained consciousness just for a moment after the injection.... But that would mean he managed to go back into a coma of his own accord...."

* * *

Daniel awakes in his room in the Archon's Tower. Eireis is waiting anxiously by his bedside.
"Here I am again," he says feeling weak. "I've been nothing but trouble." He runs his hand over his forehead. "Ouch!" He's found the large bump where the Urtikai warrior's club had connected with the side of his head. If it hadn't been for his helmet, he probably wouldn't have woken up at all.
"You were very brave, Da-ni-el," she says. "Our warriors say that you were attacked by dozens of Urtikai warriors and that you fought them valiantly. You were always to the fore, and it was only a lucky blow that knocked you out."
"I don't remember very much about fighting valiantly," he says, trying to piece together the events after he and the warriors had emerged from the tunnel. It had all happened so fast. One minute, he was in the dark and dank tunnel, the next, blinded by the bright sunlight, surrounded by screaming enemy warriors.

"If it hadn't been for Margrave, we would have been victorious." Eireis tells him about Margrave's treachery.

"Margrave?" Daniel says puzzled.

"He used the mirror on a tower overlooking the enemy camp to send a warning to the enemy, the traitor!" she says bitterly. "But you need no longer worry about Lord Keeper Margrave," she announces with satisfaction. "He's now a prisoner in the Archon's Tower, and he will be exiled from the Citadel at the Time of Going Forth."

Daniel is only half-listening to Eireis. He's remembering the other things he'd seen when he in the thick of the battle and later unconscious: his parents and grandfather in a white room, his own body lying on a bed, and a doctor and nurse standing over him. He remembers the frightened looks on their faces. "I know who I am, and where I come from!" he announces triumphantly. "And I have to find a way to get back."

"That's wonderful news, Da-ni-el!" Eireis says happily, but her something in her manner speaks of some secret sadness. A single cannon shot rings out over the Citadel. "Another attack?" Daniel asks, jumping to his feet, and picking up his sword.

"No, Da-ni-el, it is the signal for the Time of Going Forth."

* * *

Hours later, on the way home in the car, Jeff said, "Listen, dad, you don't have to go back to the nursing home. The spare room is made up, and you can borrow some of my clothes until I can fetch yours tomorrow."

"That's alright, lad. You've got enough to worry about with the boy in hospital and Caroline expecting again. The home is where I live now. It's not such a bad place once you get used to it."

"No, dad," Caroline said to clarify Jeff's words. "We're not asking you to stay the night but to come home to live with us permanently, if you'll have us, that is."

There were tears in the old man's eyes, and he was too affected to reply.

"It's what we both want, dad," Jeff said to break the silence. "What do you say?"

* * *

The scene in the Citadel is quite different from the festival atmosphere of the Calling. But once again, the whole population is engaged in a huge engineering project that takes up all their time and energy. This time, however, the Argaë work quietly, wrapped up in their hopes and fears for the future.

Daniel looks up at the sun, which is no longer directly overhead but has started its inexorable decline towards the Western horizon. There, beyond the towering fortresses of the Great Kings, the cold, inky blackness of the next Whiteday is gathering.

There, Daniel thinks, the Lethe waits in the frozen bleakness to spread its icy fingers over the Green Kingdom. Winter! He suddenly realises. That's why there's no night and day here, and why the Argaë never sleep. Greenday is our human spring, summer and autumn, when the plant world awakes, blossoms, fruits and sets it seeds, and Whiteday is the winter, when the plant kingdom sleeps. Plant kingdom... he remembers the world from his biology class or a documentary – the Green Kingdom.

Daniel follows Eireis as she tours the Citadel, visiting tower after tower, encouraging the Argaë as they toil at their latest undertaking. High above the Citadel the huge nets filled with spheres are now fully airborne. The spheres themselves have inflated to many times their original size and turned such a dark purplish-red that they look black. They bump into one another trying to escape the nets, pulling them into a giant mushroom shape with a long tail of netting that tethers them to the towers.

Balloons, Daniel thinks, they're just like hot-air balloons. The images flash through his mind again: a multi-coloured flock of giant hot-air balloons taking off all around him.

At the base of each tower the Argaë are assembling large boat-shaped constructions – only where the deck of a boat should be is a rounded roof, fitted with a line dozen sturdy mooring rings. The side of the hulls is pierced by a line of small round portholes. Daniel peers into one of the boats, through its one large central hatch, which is wide enough for two Argaë to walk in abreast. He estimates that the large cabin can accommodate up to one hundred passengers, as wells as their supplies and personal possessions. They'll sit on the widely spaces benches on either side of the central aisle and store their supplies and possessions in the nets attached along the internal walls and at either end of the craft. He also notices heavy ropes running the full-length of the cabin, now slack and resting on top of the benches – for the passengers to hold onto, he imagines. It must be a bumpy ride.

They look like boats, and they are clearly built to carry people, Daniel reasons, but they can't be boats, because there are no rivers or bodies of water anywhere near the Citadel, if you discount the moat.

"Will you drag them to a river or lake?" he asks Eireis.

"No, these are skyboats, Da-ni-el," she replies.

As soon as they've finished assembling a skyboat, the Argaë use ropes and pullies attached to the tower to haul it up, just like they had done with the circular mirrors and catapults. Teams of Argaë move from tower to tower to pull up the finished skyboats where they are attached to the balloons.

"Airships..." Daniel says to himself. "Where are they going?" he asks.

"Away from the Citadel and across the Green Kingdom," Eireis answers with a note of sadness in her voice. "They must go into the unknown, and if they are fortunate, they will find a place where they can build a new Citadel."

"And if they don't?" Daniel asks. Eireis does not reply but turns away from him. "Why can't they stay?"

"Every year our numbers increase many-fold, but there is not enough room in the Citadel for all. Those who have been chosen to remain will descend into the caverns under the Citadel, where they will sleep until the next Whiteday. But the others must leave. If they were to remain and share what food and space we have, we would grow ever weaker, until we would not have the strength to resist our enemies and we would all perish."

"Who chooses who is to go and who is to stay?"

"Do you remember the games we played? The races, the contests?" Eireis asks." Daniel nods. "One of the games was the Wheel of the Fortunate in the main square." Daniel pictures the wheel three times his own height. Its face was divided into four white sections and four red sections. "The wheel is more than just a game, Da-ni-el. On its turn is decided who leaves and who stays. White for stay and red for leave."

"And I spun the wheel," Daniel says. He still carries the small white token in his pocket. And the man had said that he had won the best of good fortunes. Now he understands what the man meant.

"You span the wheel..." Daniel says, trying to remember one event among so many. "What colour did you land on?"

Eireis holds out the palm of her hand, in which sits a small red token.

"But you are the Archon's daughter," Daniel says.

"Even the Archon must spin the wheel. He will not go this time, but I must leave the Citadel with the others at the Time of Going Forth."

"You must take mine," Daniel says, tying to give her his white token.

"No, Daniel," she replies. "You must remain here and find your way home."

"No. I'll come with you," Daniel says.

"You drew a white token, and everyone saw you do it," Eireis replies. "The Lore forbids that you should go. My father will not allow you to leave."

"But—" Daniel begins.

"No, Da-ni-el. The Unseen Ones said that you could not stay here and survive another Whiteday. You must find a way home before the Argaë go down into the caverns. Out there, she said indicating the plain, there is nothing but hardship, danger and death." She will not listen to anymore of his arguments of pleading. "Come," she says. "'I have a lot to do."

* * *

Caroline and Dan peered into the back garden. The canes of the briar were so heavy with berries that they were being dragged downwards. Most had already matured to dark-purple ripeness.

"Bumper crop this year," Caroline said.

Dan senior reached out and picked one and tasted it. "Iris liked blackberries," he said with a faraway look in his eyes. "We'd go picking in the summertime."

It was the first time Caroline had heard Dan mention his wife, dead these past five years. She'd always thought of their marriage as unhappy. Though more because that's what Jeff had told her so. She was a quiet woman, who never complained and always deferred to her husband in everything. But now she was seeing another side to their relationship that maybe Jeff had never seen.

"She had lots of recipes: blackberry jelly, blackberry crumble, blackberry cordial," Dan said. "They're probably in the attic somewhere."

"I'll ask Jeff to have a look for them," Caroline said. Then she added shyly, "Do you miss Iris, Dan?"

He looked thoughtful for a moment, and then replied, "Yes, lass. I do."

* * *

The Argaë work tirelessly. It seems that half the city is being dismantled and packed into the skyboats. The materials to build the boats are also taken from the towers.

Eireis is too busy with the preparations to spend much time with Daniel, so he is left alone to roam the outer edges of the Citadel. Peering over the ramparts, he surveys the plain once more. As ever the kingdom is bustling with activity, but its nature has changed. The armies that once marched across the plain have vanished. Their engines of war – catapults, trebuchets and siege towers – lie abandoned or are being dismantled so that their parts can be re-used.

All over the plain, preparations are being made for the Time of Going Forth. There are other airships of all shapes, sizes and design: huge orange and grey cigar-shaped dirigibles, each carrying a gondola large enough to carry the population of an entire village, small balloons and kites just large enough to hold one family, and every size in between, but there also stranger crafts – gliders, rockets, and helicopters – whose means of propulsion are a mystery to Daniel.

– 14 –

The Cloud Beasts

Daniel pulls his hood down over his face and follows the file of Argaë into the skyboat. The passengers are tightly packed in the cramped interior, surrounded by their bundled possessions. He sees Eireis at the front of the cabin next to the pilot. Daniel sits in a vacant seat in the front row, directly behind hers.

"Welcome, friends," she says greeting the boarding passengers; she barely spares Daniel a glance. The mood is sombre, the passengers, subdued and silent. She turns back to the pilot who is explaining the controls of the skyboat. These are few and simple: a central wheel turns the rudders that help steer the boat in the air, and levers operate flaps that can slow it down.

"The ailerons are small, but in the heights, they can be set to turn the craft from right to left, and up or down," the pilot explains. "These are for our descent," he says pointing to a series of levers set in the ceiling of the cabin above the pilot's seat. "When the balloon is detached from the skyboat, these will deploy the wings so that the skyboats glides down to earth and lands safely."

Daniel listens carefully but keeps his head down and his hood low over his face. He doesn't want to break his cover and reveal his identity to Eireis as he's sure that if she's able to, she'll force him to disembark.

At last, the skyboat is fully laden, the hatches are closed and tied shut with cords, and the gangplanks linking it to the tower are removed.

"Unfasten the moorings," the pilot calls to the Argaë on the tower.

At his command, the ropes that hold the skyboat level with the top of the tower are released. The passengers cry out in fear as the skyboat shakes itself free of its moorings and begins to rise, slowly at first. The speed of the skyboat's ascent increases, and Daniel feels a sickening lurching sensation in his stomach as the one remaining mooring rope takes the strain. The skyboat comes to a sudden halt, swaying alarmingly in the gathering wind on the end of its single tether.

Daniel looks out of the small porthole. Skyboats hang by thin umbilical cords from every tower at different heights so as to minimize the danger of collisions. They sway gently in the wind, which is still no more than a gentle breeze.

There is to be no Calling this time. The Unseen Ones coming this time are not the beautiful creatures of multi-coloured tracery that filled the sky during the ceremony on the Archon's Tower. Daniel remembers the pictures of terrible monsters in the Tower of the Lore and a sense of dread fills his heart. The Cloud Beasts, they're called. For a moment, he regrets his rash decision to follow Eireis. But then he reproaches himself for his cowardice. Why should he be safe within the walls of the Citadel while she is forced to face the Cloud Beasts and heaven knows what other dangers.

The sky in the west is filled with boiling black clouds. The wind is getting stronger by the minute, tossing the skyboats violently as it gusts around the towers. The pilot tries to steady the craft, but there is little he can do while it remains tethered.

"Eireis..." Daniel whispers.

She turns at the familiar voice. "Da-ni-el!" she gasps. "What are you doing here? You don't know the dangers you're exposing yourself to."

"I couldn't stay while you went."

"But we may never reach safety to create another Citadel."

Eireis turns to the pilot. "Can you take the skyboat back down to the tower?" she asks.

"My Lady—" the pilot begins, but just then a violent gust of wind sends the boat tumbling across the sky, almost snapping the cord that holds it.

"The Cloud Beasts!" an Argaë cries out in terror.

Hideous shapes emerge from the clouds. They are huge: many times bigger than the skyboats and their balloons. They have wings so dark, they seem to be made of black smoke, and in the centre, a pair of fiery red eyes and a gaping circular maw full of fangs. They flap around the fragile fleet and snap at the balloons and tethers. Their wings scythe through the air as and slice through the ropes that hold the skyboats to the towers.

Daniel hears a sharp crack as the balloon is wrenched free from its last mooring. It spirals upwards as the pilot fights to regain control.

"Watch out!" Daniel cries out as another boat collides with them. It strikes the front of the skyboat, tearing a gash through the fragile wicker skin. Despite the safety rope that holds the passengers to the floor of the skyboat, the pilot is flung into the darkness, his terrified screams instantly swallowed by the roars of the Cloud Beasts.

Daniel grabs Eireis by the waist with one arm as he holds on to the side of the skyboat with the other. The craft spins wildly out of control. He must get to the controls. He unfastens the rope around his waist and signals Eireis to get behind him. He leaps into the pilot's empty seat. The craft pitches forwards almost throwing him out, then rolls back the other way. He grabs hold of the rope on the floor and manages to tie himself to it. Sometimes climbing, sometimes falling towards the control, he makes it to the pilot's seat. He halls back on the wheel with all his strength and manages to bring the skyboat back to level flight. He pulls the levers to lower the flaps to slow it down. He succeeds in stabilizing the craft. Immediately the passengers set to work to repair the damaged side of the craft with whatever comes to hand.

But there is no time for rejoicing or congratulations. The Cloud Beasts swoop down on the balloons, as if they were playing with them.

"What do they want with us?" Daniel shouts to be heard above the terrible din of the storm and the screeching of the beasts.

"These Unseen Ones don't know us. I cannot speak to them nor see into their minds. I don't understand their purpose but without them we cannot travel away from the Citadel to seek a new home."

Daniel looks down to the Citadel far below. Only a few balloons remain tethered to the towers. The towers themselves are taking a terrible battering. Many lie shattered, while others sway precipitously. All over the plain, buildings are smashed and wrecked by the terrible wings of the Cloud Beasts and the storms that they generate. No construction, no matter how strong, seems immune from their terrible power.

The Argaë are not the only tribe to have taken to the skies. In the flashes of lightning that illuminate the blackness, Daniel can make out hundreds of crafts, from large cigar-shaped dirigibles and huge gliders ferrying hundreds, to wing-shaped kites carrying no more than one family and flocks of parachutes, each carrying one person each.

The storm is at its peak. The howls of the Cloud Beasts make all attempts at conversation impossible. All Daniel can do was hold on to the controls and try to steer as level a course as he can.

One of the Cloud Beasts is making straight for the boat. Its bulk soon fills the whole sky in front of them. The beast opens its jaws wide, and roars. Daniel braces himself, expecting the great teeth to crunch up the skyboat and its passengers, but it flies past them and into a dark tunnel. All movement and noise cease.

* * *

Dan senior was sitting contently in his garden once more. Jeff had bought him a new deckchair to replace the one that had rotted away, and Caroline was always fussing over him, asking him if he was warm enough, or wanted a cup of tea. September had been kind so far, and the days, though shorter, were still warm and fine. With Caroline's help, he'd restored the lawn, ridding it of all but its most stubborn patches of moss, and cleared the beds ready for planting next spring. The back garden, they had so far left mostly untouched. Jeff and Dan senior had cleared a rough path through the centre of the briar, so that they could reach the pond, fruit cage and shed. They had created more paths into the briar by pressing the canes down.

The crop of blackberries had more than made up for the absence of the soft f fruit that Dan senior grew every year. Caroline had collected them by the bucketload, so that they were now heartily sick of blackberry tarts and crumbles. She was planning to turn the remainder of the crop into jam and summer puddings that she would freeze for the winter. No matter how many she picked and the birds ate, there always seemed to be more. She wondered at the profligacy of nature. Most humans managed two or three offspring in their lifetimes, but plants seemed to produce them by the millions.

Dan senior had found the old hive at the back of the orchard, now long abandoned by the colony, the wood rotting and covered with mould. The bees still came into the garden, of course, to collect nectar from the wildflowers, but they were from a wild colony somewhere in the small patch of woodland beyond the garden wall. It was likely that it was an offshoot of his colony, and that its queen was a descendant of the queens he had reared.

He watched the insects as they collected the last of the year's bounty. Soon they would return to the hive and make ready for the winter. The useless drone males would be expelled, and the colony would settle to wait out the cold, keeping warm by congregating in the centre of the hive around the queen. Many would die, he knew. Because natural colonies were even more vulnerable to damage and attack than manmade ones, but the queen usually survived.

A lone bee left her nectar collection duties and flew lazily towards him in the staggering, uncertain flight that bees used to confuse predators. It circled above him a few times and then landed on his hand. Dan senior stared at it puzzled. Bees sometimes investigated humans just in case they might be some kind of giant exotic flower, but they didn't stay long, unlike wasps, which seemed to delight in harassing them. He hated wasps as much as the bees did. Wasps and bees looked similar but they were deadly enemies. The wasps were destroyers and predators who raided the colonies, killed the queen and her workers and devoured the brood.

The bee tilted her body up to face him and began to dance. He had seen bees dance many times. It was the way they communicated with one another. The workers would arrive laden with nectar and pollen at the hive and tell their waiting sisters where to fly to. Tiny movements of the body, legs and antennae indicated directions, wind speed, types of nectar and pollen and a hundred other piece of information that the other bees needed to know.

"Watch out, dad!" Caroline said alarmed. "It'll sting you!" She swatted ineffectually at the bee, which flew off back towards the flowers.

"It was a bee," he told her. "They won't sting unless they're attacked."

Jeff had offered to buy another hive, but Caroline had been dead set against it with the new baby on the way.

The Emerald Path

The skyboat is in total darkness. One by one, the Argaë light the little storm lamps that they have brought with them. The weak flames create little pools of light in the otherwise oppressive blackness.

"Where are we?" Daniel asks.

"In the belly of the cloud beast," Eireis replies. "They devour the skyboats and carry us far and wide over the Green Kingdom."

Daniel wants to ask how long they will be held prisoners within the beast, but he knows that such questions don't have any meaning in the Green Kingdom, where time is measured in a different way. Without the cycle of night and day or the seasons of his world – the Red Kingdom – time is marked by the ceremonies of the Green Kingdom: the Re-building, the Calling and the Time of Setting Forth, and the rhythm of Greenday and Whitedays, the seasons of life, growth and fruiting, and of deathlike hibernation through the bleak cold of winter.

Daniel and the Argaë fall into a trance as they travel inside the cloud beast. He does not know if hours or days of his own time have passed when the light floods into the skyboat from every side.

They are flying through the air again high above the kingdom but without the balloon that carried them before they are losing height fast.

"The wings, Da-ni-el! You must deploy the wings," Eireis cries out.

Daniel reaches up to the levers the pilots had shown Eireis but they are stuck and refuse to move.

"Help him!" Eireis instructs the Argaë nearest to him.

Together Daniel, Eireis and the Argaë manage to wrench the levers free. A series of creaks shake the frame of the skyboat as its roof opens up into two halves. The roof sections slide back on pulleys and begin to rotate to create two long V-shaped wings. The wings catch the updraft and the craft slows and levels out as the wings are fully extended.

Daniel is exhilarated to find that he is flying the skyboat like the glider his father had taken him up on his eighth birthday. But then he had been able to recognize familiar landmarks: villages, woods and the checkerboard of fields, crisscrossed with roads dotted with cars and trucks no bigger than his toys. Here above the plain, there are no landmarks, no buildings or roads.

"Where do I land?" he asks Eireis.

Eireis, her hair whipped up by the wind, looks out over the plain, and points. "That way, Da-ni-el. Can you not see?" she asks her voice full of exultation. "Can you not see the Emerald Road in the sky that guides us down to the plain?"

Daniel stares ahead. All he can see is the sky and the plain beneath. As hard as he looks, he cannot see anything that might be an Emerald Road. Eireis holds his hand. "Close your eyes, Da-ni-el," she says. "Look through my eyes."

Daniel closes his eyes. He can see the plain and sky as before, but the land is veined like a giant leaf, shot through with filaments of iridescent green and blue. "Can you see now?" Eireis asks.

"Yes, I can see them. They're so beautiful," he replies.

"Do you see our Emerald Path now? Follow where it leads and land the skyboat where it ends, Da-ni-el."

As the glider loses height, the sky is full of other flying crafts, Argaë gliders among them, each following a separate glowing trail down to the plain below.

"Look there!" she points to the place where the Emerald Path emerges from the earth. "That's where we shall make our new home."

Remembering his own flight with his father, Daniel realises that he will have to circle around their intended landing site to lose speed and put the skyboat down safely. He pulls the flaps down on one side and turns the rudders to the right, sending them into a banking turn. Each turn gets them lower and closer to the desired landing spot. All about them, other crafts are making their landings – some gracefully and slowly on giant parachutes, others so sudden and violent that Daniel wonders how anyone could survive so strong an impact.

"We're about to land!" Daniel warns his passengers. "Hold on tight!"

The New Citadel

From the pilot's viewpoint, the ground speeds upwards to meet the falling skyboat. Even with its ailerons fully deployed, as the pilot had explained to Eireis, the skyboat is descending at a dizzying speed. The passengers cry out in fear and cling tightly to one another and to the thick rope that runs the length of the cabin.

"Stay calm, my friends" Eireis says, trying to comfort them. "We have the noble and brave Da-ni-el who lives in the Sky at the controls! He'll make sure no harm comes to us."

Daniel smiles at her barefaced lie, but he does not share her confidence in his ability to land the skyboat in one piece, but her words seem to reassure the passengers. What would King Edmund do? he wonders. Harry Potter would have a spell about his person, and if he didn't, the ever-dependable Hermione would provide one. Once again, he thinks it's hard to live up to his fictional heroes. But why should he even try? After all, it's not as if they're real and had done any of the things in the films.

Close up, the ground looks a lot more uneven than it did from the air. Following the Emerald Path is no longer a problem, because at this height it's so broad that the skyboat is flying within it.

"Look over there," Eireis says in an awed voice, pointing to the right of the skyboat. "The fortresses of the Great Kings."

They are flying within sight of the gigantic fortresses with dark, forbidding walls and towers. Each is much larger than the whole Argaë citadel. It's the first time Daniel has had a chance to see them close up. He scans the battlements, towers and courtyards but can see no signs of life. Whoever the Great Kings are, they keep themselves well hidden.

The path veers away from the fortresses towards an area of more level ground. But immediately beyond the landing site, a sheer cliff rises a hundred feet. It's going to be a tight landing, otherwise, he risks crashing into the cliff if he mistimes it. All around them other crafts are landing, some smoothly, others corkscrewing into the ground, so that they bury themselves as soon as they land.

All too fast, the moment of truth has come for the skyboat and its novice pilot. The nose of the skyboat hits the ground but bounces up straight away.

This is it, Daniel thinks. "Hold on to something!" he calls out.

The skyboat does not have landing gear like the glider Daniel flew in with his father, but the bottom of the "hull" is V-shaped so that it will cut through the soft ground as it lands. He prays there are no boulders or buried rocks in their path. He tries to keep the nose up, as he remembers his father doing, so that the craft comes down level. The impact as it hits the ground for the second time jars every bone in Daniel's body. The passengers and their possessions are thrown around the cabin, as the boat skids along the ground sending great clods of earth and grass into the air. The cliff is looming up in front of them. We won't stop in time! he thinks in a panic. We'll all be killed, and it will be my fault!

At that moment, the right side of the hull hits a half-buried rock, and the skyboat is thrown into the air at an angle; the left wing digs itself into the ground, making the boat veer wildly to the left. The left wing snaps off, and the boat is free again, this time sliding with the remaining right wing straight towards the cliff. The skyboat tears up the ground side on. If it weren't for the wing, the skyboat would have rolled towards the cliff to their certain deaths. As it is, the wing smashes into the cliff, bringing the craft to a shuddering halt.

Inside the cabin all is confusion and noise. "Is everyone alright?" Daniel asks, trying to make himself heard over the din. He unties himself and Eireis, and together they make their way to the back of the craft. Helping up the fallen and stunned and checking the injured.

"Carry out the injured first," Eireis orders.

Their accustomed discipline returns to the Argaë. The terror and panic forgotten, they attend to the matters at hand. The injured must be cared for, the stores unloaded and a fortified stockade built. They know there's no time to lose. The next Whiteday is not far off, and there is much to be done before the Argaë are able to sleep safe in their new home.

* * *

The day had come for Jeff to fetch Dan senior home. For the first time in his life, Jeff realised, he was actually enjoying spending time with his father. It was a strange feeling after all those years of unspoken resentment and grudging respect. Dan senior's attitude to his son, too, had changed. They now hugged when they met – still a little self-consciously – but it was a start.

Caroline had redecorated the bedroom that she had intended to be Daniel's room when he became a teenager, as it was at the back of the house on the ground floor and had French windows opening onto the garden. She had furnished it with some of the pieces Dan senior had left behind and decorated with personal items – photographs and knick-knacks that had belonged to the old man and his wife. She had had his suits dry-cleaned and had washed and ironed his dress shirts.

Now that Dan senior was back at Greenacres, he could spend more time with his grandson in hospital. Caroline dropped him off in the morning, so that he could sit with Daniel, and then she'd come and join him in the afternoon. They chatted a little, but more often than not, they sat together in silence,

Caroline knitting while Dan senior read the paper or watched daytime TV.

* * *

Daniel is among the last to jump out of the skyboat. He takes a look around the landing site. The ground is rocky, with a few large boulders that look as if they have fallen from the cliff. No other craft, Argaë nor from any another tribe, has landed nearby, though in the distance he can see the palisade of an Urtikai encampment being built.

The Argaë immediately set to work. Nothing is wasted. The skyboat is dismantled until the wooden planks and wicker partitions of the fuselage and wings, and the coils of rope are all stacked and ready to be re-used. A party is sent out to collect the broken wing and any other debris lost during the landing. Everything is added to the neat piles; even the nails are removed and straightened, ready for re-use. As usual, Daniel feels surplus to requirements. There is no role for him, and the Argaë, now fully recovered from the ordeal of the flight, work methodically and quickly.

Once the skyboat has been dismantled, the Argaë gather respectfully around one of their number. He's tall for an Argaë and wears dark-green tunic, leggings and cloak. He's dressed as a loremaster, and Daniel is immediately suspicious of him. But the man has not even looked in his direction. He is busy with preparations of his own.

"He's the Dowser," Eireis whispers to him. He holds what looks like a tree branch whittled bare of any twigs and leaves at arms' length. Looking closer, Daniel sees that the stick is shaped like a letter Y. The Dowser holds one of the shorter angled arms of the Y in each hand and points the Y's tail in front of him. Beginning from the place where the skyboat landed, the Dowser walks in a spiral pattern as if he were following an invisible path. He proceeds slowly, but all of a sudden, he veers wildly to the left, swerving from his original path, as if it were the stick that was pulling him forwards. Daniel bursts out laughing because it looks as if the whole performance is some kind of elaborate show put on to entertain the onlookers, but one look at the tense faces of the Argaë tells him that they believe that what the Dowser is doing is deadly serious.

He staggers forward, almost falling with every other step, so strong is the attraction from the dowsing rod. He's being drawn to a spot twenty or thirty paces from the landing site. He comes to a halt in a small hollow, where the rod is wrenched from the Dowser's hands and sticks upright, tail-first, in the ground. He looks up triumphantly. At once, the Argaë begin to move their stores and the dismantled parts of the skyboat towards the spot the rod has indicated. In minutes they've built a dome from the wicker outer hull of the skyboat over the hollow. Another group use axes to carve points in both ends of the wooden planks and posts. Under the dome a team of Argaë has already started digging, while another carries the excavated soil to create a rampart around the deepening hole, and a third is assembling a sturdy scaffolding directly above the diggers within the wicker dome. So, this is the birth of a new Citadel, Daniel thinks.

He watches as a wicker basket large enough to hold a dozen Argaë is hung from a system of pulleys attached to the framework above the deepening well. Coils of heavy rope indicate that the basket can be lowered a considerable distance. The diggers in the well, he sees, have ropes tied around their waists, although thus far, the walls of the well are not even above their heads.

"What are they looking for?" Daniel asks Eireis, unable to contain his curiosity.

"They are seeking out a new cavern where we may sleep during the coming Whiteday, Da-ni-el," she replies. "We must be safely asleep by the time the Lethe returns to the Green Kingdom." She looks thoughtfully at him. "What will you do?"

"I don't think I can share the sleep of the Argaë," Daniel replies sadly. "I must find a way back to the Red Kingdom. I don't think I'll be able to survive the whole of Whiteday alone." He remembers the bitter cold and darkness, and the beguiling voice of the Lethe as it hunted him across the bleak, frozen landscape.

"I wish I could help you get back home, Da-ni-el," Eireis begins. "But my knowledge is limited.

Maybe the Great Kings would be able to counsel you." Eireis has mentioned them before in passing as the mightiest and wisest beings of the Green Kingdom.

"I thought you said they were terrible," Daniel says looking towards the horizon where the fortresses of the Great Kings they had flown over loom over the plain.

"No, they're not monsters," she corrects him. "But so great is their power that they sometimes overlook the existence of the kingdom's lesser tribes."

A great shout goes up within the wicker dome. The diggers, Daniel notices, are nowhere to be seen. And now he understands why they had ropes tied around their waists. The bottom of the well they were digging has suddenly given way and they have fallen through into an underground chasm.

"Is all safe?" an Argaë shouts down to the miners.

After a short pause, a series of shouts are heard from the darkness, as the miners call out their replies. They're hauled up one by one. Suspended on rope harnesses, the miners work furiously to enlarge the hole so that it can accommodate the full width of the wicker basket.

Deep below, Daniel knows, there's a cavern that one day will be as large as the one where he first encountered the Argaë. The basket is quickly filled with timbers from the skyboat that the Argaë will use to build ladders to get down from the surface and props for the passages that they'll dig down to the cavern. The basket is slowly lowered into the darkness. Daniel wonders how long it will be before they have decorated every inch of the tunnels with the painted bas-reliefs that he saw in the passageways of the cavern under the Archon's Tower. And next Greenday, the first of many more towers will rise. This will be the foundation of the Archon's Tower of the new citadel.

A chill wind begins to blow from the West, bringing with it an intimation of the icy darkness to come.

"It's the fourth quarter. Greenday will soon end, Da-ni-el," Eireis says. "We must begin our descent into the cavern. Come, let's see what they've found."

The basket has to make several trips to carry enough timber to build a ladder up to the surface. Eireis and Daniel climb into the basket, which is already fully laden with supplies and Argaë carrying the tools they had brought with them in the skyboat. The order is given and the two stout poles holding the basket are removed. It swings over the void as the ropes take the slack. Two teams of a dozen Argaë let out the ropes that lower the basket down into the well. The lanterns hanging on the sides of the basket cast a weak glow onto the featureless earthen sides. After a relatively short descent, the basket reaches the bottom. The Argaë climb out and immediately set to work on making ladders up to the surface.

A tunnel opens to one side; its entrance has already been enlarged by the miners, who have propped up walls and ceiling. Lanterns spaced every ten paces light their way to where the Argaë, led again by the Dowser, are excavating to make the tunnel high enough to walk through without stooping. Smaller galleries open to the right and left of the tunnel they're following. But it's clear that they are no longer in need of the Dowser's guidance to find what they seek. The smell of water is so strong in the confined space of the tunnel that everyone there – even Daniel – can follow it.

"But who made these tunnels?" Daniel asks Eireis.

"There are many tribes of Unseen Ones, Da-ni-el," she explains. "Those of the sky and those of the earth. We cannot—"

"We have broken through!" a man shouts, interrupting Eireis's explanation.

The pair runs to the spot where a moment earlier, there had been an opening barely large enough for Chirrip to enter. Daniel can sense that the miners have broken through to a much larger space, as yet still shrouded in darkness.

An Argaë with a rope tied around his waist steps forwards with a lantern and edges out into the darkness. The light he carries casts a gigantic shadow across the vast cavernous space. The moment of truth has come. They know they've found water, but is there enough to create a new citadel? The Dowser begins the arduous climb down into the cavern. He slips and loses his footing several times and is only saved because of the safety rope tied around his waist.

* * *

A van pulled up in front of the house. Two men got out, and while one unloaded the equipment, the other went to ring the doorbell. The man and Caroline had a conversation on the doorstep. Taking one look at his muddy boots and the equipment that was being unloaded, she pointed to the path that went along the side of the house into the garden.

The sign on the van read: "Michael Meek, Landscape Gardener. No job too big, no job too small."

The Water Eireis

The tiny lantern that the Dowser carries is quickly lost in the darkness as he descends into the depths of the cavern, lowered on the end of the rope. For what seems an eternity to the waiting Argaë, there's no sound from the blackness except for the creak of the rope, which suddenly goes slack. Has the rope snapped, sending the dowser to his death or has he reached solid ground? A few moments later, the Argaë feel a series of tugs on the rope that signal that he is safe and has reached his goal.

"The Pool of Life! The Pool of Life!" Their words and cheers echo around the tunnels into the caverns below.

Now that they have reached water, the migration from the surface can begin in earnest. The feverish pitch of activity will not diminish until all the Argaë and their supplies are safely underground. At a speed that Daniel finds dizzying, they set to work to cut a flight of steps down to the cavern floor and level the area around the Pool of Life in its centre, building a neat circular pool with smooth sides. Another group have drilled a narrow vertical shaft to the surface so that a column of grey light penetrates the cavern and illuminates the pool at its centre. He sees that everything is ready for Whiteday.

* * *

"It's a big job," Michael Meek said to Caroline as they surveyed the rear garden and the tangles of brambles that still filled most of the available space. Apart from clearing a central path, Dan and Jeff had done little to control canes in the rest of the rear garden, and even where they had been cut back, they were beginning to sprout fresh growth.

"They're a devil for spreading. We'll have to get all of it out, roots and all, otherwise you'll get it back by next spring," Michael Meek said as he rolled a cigarette deftly with one hand, licked and pasted it into a slightly squashed cylinder, and lit it with a match. Instead of snuffing out the match, he let the tiny yellow flame burn until it guttered out between his callused fingers. "No wind," he said. "Fetch the flame-thrower, there's a good lad," he said to Norbert, his assistant.

He looked up at the sky and sniffed. There was rain in the air, but it wouldn't be until later in the afternoon, he thought. Time enough to clear most of the back garden.

* * *

A violent tremor rocks the cave, loosening part of the ceiling and flinging the Argaë to the ground.

But as quickly as it had struck, the earthquake is stilled.

"What was that?" Daniel asks Eireis.

"With the coming of Whiteday, the tribes of the Green Kingdom are not the only ones that seek shelter underground," Eireis replies. "There are many Unseen Ones that also descend into the earth."

"And can they do you harm?"

"Do you remember the pictures you saw in the Tower of the Lore?" she asks in a whisper so no one else can hear her.

"The ones of the Cloud Beasts?" Daniel remembers the pictures of fearsome monsters inside which they have travelled to reach the Cavern. Many were of the air, but there had been others, with tentacles, claws and mouths full of jagged teeth....

"There are many Unseen Ones, Da-ni-el. Some know us, others do not, but many can destroy us. We are not safe until we lie in sleep in the crystals." Then she adds, "And even then, there are still dangers for us."

Daniel looks around. For the first time since he arrived in the Citadel, he notices that the Argaë are still; they stand silently in small groups, waiting for something. He realises that he has never seen them inactive for any length of time. The cavern has been made ready, the stores have been put away, and the tunnels and shafts to the surface propped and stabilized. For the first time, there's nothing for them to do.

At an unseen signal from Eireis, the Argaë colonists stand in concentric circles around the Pool of Life. They are dressed in their best clothes and carry their tools and weapons: the workers in cloaks of sliver-green threads over their jerkins; the warriors resplendent in their helmets, polished armour and gleaming shields and spears. Daniel remembers his visit to the cavern beneath the Archon's Tower and the Urtikai's attack. They sleep but are prepared to fight and work as soon as they wake up.

This year they stand a few dozen-strong, but next year, Daniel imagines, they'll be hundreds. Their numbers will fill the floor of the cavern until they need to create tiers along the walls, and finally build galleries extending up to the cavern's high roof. In a few years, there will be thousands of Argaë in this new citadel, filling this and many other underground caverns.

Eireis steps forward to the edge of the pool. She holds up her arms and begins to sing a single clear note. Points of light sparkle at the centre of the pool, whose waters begin to bubble and churn. A column of water rises from the pool and grows until it is the same height as Eireis. But the apparition is not the one that Daniel had seen during his visit to the Tower of the Lore. That figure had been shapeless – a mere suggestion of a human figure. To Daniel's amazement, the watery column takes on Eireis's exact appearance – recreating every detail of her face and clothing but in crystal-clear water. The Water Eireis takes up the note that Eireis is singing and modulates it, until the two callers are singing in harmony.

Daniel watches in fascination as the Water Eireis extends her arms over Eireis's head until they reach the Argaë standing around them. The Argaë disappear in the swirling ribbons of water emanating from the Pool of Life, but instead of drenching the Argaë, it solidifies into green and blue crystal sarcophagi as it settles around their bodies. In a matter of seconds, the sarcophagi are complete. The Water Eireis pulls back the ribbons of water into herself. She stands silent in the centre of the pool.

Eireis suddenly cries out in pain and staggers, about to fall.

Daniel rushes to her side. "What's happening?" he asks.

"A terrible disaster..." she says, her voice a little more than a whisper. "I can feel great heat. The Citadel is under attack."

Daniel catches hold of her to stop her from falling and is suddenly overcome by an intense burning sensation that comes not from Eireis but somehow through her.

"The Citadel is burning..." Eireis whispers.

For a moment, she cannot speak. "It has stopped..." she gasps. The heat that Daniel felt through her body slowly fades.

"How do you know?" Daniel asks.

"Even when I am not in the Citadel, I am part of it," she explains. "What they sense, I can sense also."

* * *

"Norbert, not the green stuff!" Michael Meek said in an exasperated tone. "The dry canes underneath." Norbert pointed the flame-thrower towards the base of the briar. "Short bursts. We're here to clear the garden not incinerate it!"

Norbert hesitantly pressed the button again and a jet of flame leapt towards the dried canes closest to him. The canes exploded into red and yellow flame but the greener material was still wet from the rain, and the fire did not take hold. Caroline stepped out of the kitchen with a tray of tea and biscuits.

"Hold up, lad" Michael Meek told Norbert.

The boy lowered the flame-thrower. The burn he'd started was already petering out.

"Bit damp with all the rain we've had this week," Michael Meek said taking the proffered mug of tea and a biscuit.

The sky was suddenly overcast, with heavy rain clouds gathering from the east. Michael Meek looked up. "Put it back in the van, Norbert. There's a good lad."

"Any chance of you coming back tomorrow?" Caroline asked.

"'Fraid not, love" Michael Meek replied. "Got a big job in Mortimer Crescent. It'll have to be next week or the week after. I'll give you a bell."

For reasons that she couldn't fathom, Caroline was relieved that the two men hadn't been able to clear the back garden. The briar was too big, of course, but it had provided the family, garden birds and field mice and squirrels with a bounty of blackberries, and the thistles, nettles and bramble flowers had attracted butterflies and bees all spring and summer. She had half a dozen jars of jam and jelly and big tubs full of berries in the freezer. She wondered if there might be a way of keeping part of the briar.

"Leave it," Norbert had explained, "and it'll take over the garden again in no time. They're terrible for spreading."

"Well, if you really think so," she said uncertainly. There was something nagging away at her, but she couldn't quite put her finger on it. "I suppose there are plenty more over there," she said looking over the back wall at the small area of woodland beyond.

* * *

Eireis and Daniel are now the only two awake in the cavern. The Water Eireis looks at Daniel with curiosity. "You are not of the Argaë, yet you are not of the tribes of Unseen Ones that I have seen in the depths of the Green Kingdom," she says. "What manner of creature are you?"

Daniel explains what he knows about his origins in terms that the Water Eireis will understand and asks her if she knows how he can return to the Red Kingdom. The Water Caller turns her crystal gaze downwards. Shapes some sleek and beautiful, others gnarled and hideous rise and subside in the water at her feet. It's as if she were consulting some record of things long past. After a moment, she looks up and says sadly, "I am sorry but I cannot help you, stranger."

"I, too, must sleep, Da-ni-el," Eireis says, her voice noticeably weaker.

A sudden iciness grasps Daniel's heart. He'll be all alone again, just like during his first days in the Green Kingdom – alone in the desolation of ice and at the mercy of the Lethe. If he cannot find his way back home, will he be able to survive Whiteday on his own?

"I have a parting gift to you," Eireis says, taking a small bag that hung from her belt. It floats in his hands, because its contents seem to be slightly lighter than the surrounding air. He begins to unfasten the tie that holds it closed. "No do not open it, Da-ni-el, for you can only open it once, and then its power will be spent."

"What does it do?" he asks.

But Eireis no longer seems to be able to hear or see him. She turns away from him and stands close by the Pool of Life, in the place of honour where the Archon had stood in the other cavern where Daniel had first seen the Argaë. The Water Eireis stretches out her arms once more and embraces Eireis within ribbons of water that solidify around her as he watches.

"Don't leave me!" he whispers.

Eireis seems to see him again, just for one brief moment, though only with a great effort. "You are strong and brave, Da-ni-el, you will find a way to return to the Red Kingdom.... Remember me, as I will remember you always..." she says, her voice trailing away. He closes his eyes and when he opens them again, Eireis is encased inside her sarcophagus in the deep sleep of Whiteday. The Water Eireis smiles at him and begins to dissolve into the Pool of Life.

"No! Don't leave," he implores her. But she, too, sinks back into the pool. He watches the water until it is completely still. The surface of the pool becomes like a silver mirror. The face he sees reflected in it is anxious and tearful – a mask of sadness and despair.

"You've been in worst scrapes," he says to himself aloud. He recalls his many adventures among the Argaë: the fall into the Underworld, the battle with the Urtikai – he's managed to survive them all unscathed. Be brave, like Harry, Ron, Hermione and all the other brave children from his favourite movies, he tells himself. But they had each other, and I'm alone. He attaches Eireis' strange present to his belt, still wondering what it can do. It is lighter than air, so maybe it will allow him to fly, he thinks. He walks up to Eireis's crystal and kisses the cold glassy surface over her face. "Goodbye," he says.

He turns his back on the crystals and climbs the stairs and ladders back to the surface. The sky is a darkening shade of grey and the air, cool. A chill wind is rising from the West. He turns towards the fortresses of the Great Kings and starts to walk.

The Citadel Burns

In the Citadel, the remaining Argaë are making their preparations for Whiteday. Household goods and stores of food and anything that might be of use for the next Greenday are carried underground. The Argaë are already feeling sluggish because of the cold. They work slowly and with increasing difficulty. In the fourth quadrant all social differences are forgotten, and warriors, courtiers, loremasters, even the Archon himself, work side by side with the workers and artisans. The repairs to the towers and city walls are no longer carried out, and from time to time, pieces of carved masonry come crashing onto the walkways, their intricate painted reliefs shattering as they hit the ground. Soon the Citadel's streets will be empty, the haunt of the Lethe for the Whiteday to come.

"Hurry, my people, hurry," the Archon encourages his subjects. "Soon the darkness will be upon us."

* * *

Michael Meek's van was outside the house again. His big job in Mortimer Crescent had not been to be so big after all. He and Norbert were unloading the equipment they'd need to clear out the back garden once and for all: the flamethrower and the rotovator that they only needed for the really big jobs.

"Got to get all the roots out, you see," Michael told his assistant Norbert. "The briar, the nettles, the thistles – they'll just sit underground and come back next year twice as bad if you don't get them all out."

* * *

In the other crystal cavern far from the Citadel, Eireis sleeps, but her sleep is troubled. She's standing on top of the Archon's Tower. She remembers being here once before during another Whiteday sleep; but was it last Whiteday or one hundred Whitedays before? She cannot tell.

"This isn't real," she says out loud. The air shimmers in front of her. The Unseen One manifests herself in the Green Kingdom, twisting the air into its shape.

"A great calamity approaches," she warns. "But this time, dream and reality will be as one. You must find Da-ni-el. Only he can stop this. Find Da-ni-el..." the Invisible One repeats as she fades out of existence.

* * *

Michael ignited the flamethrower with his lighter.

"No, like I showed you last week," he instructed the hapless Norbert. "Start at the bottom with the dry stuff, and it'll burn up the green stuff, no problem. And don't give it too much welly, lad," he warned, but he had a fire extinguisher at the ready just in case. "We don't want to burn the house down, do we?"

There previous few days had been rain-free, and the canes had had a chance to dry out. Using the paths that Dan and Jeff had made for Caroline's blackberry picking expeditions in the summer, Norbert worked his way through the briar, methodically following Michael's instructions.

* * *

The Citadel is burning!

Huge fireballs come crashing out of the sky smashing into the towers and ramparts. Soon the whole circuit of the walls and the outer edges of the city are alight and the fire moves inexorably inwards towards the Archon's Tower and the Tower of the Lore. The Archon rallies his people, trying to lead them to safety but quickly realises that there is no place of safety left on the surface.

"Abandon anything that you cannot carry!" he orders. "Into the underground passages and down into the caverns! There we will be safe from the fire!"

The panicked Argaë are calmed by his words and quickly obey his orders. They drop their heavy packs and abandon their carts and animals and rush into the nearest towers and file down into the tunnels that lead into the underground caverns.

* * *

Horrified, Eireis witnesses the scene from the top of the Archon's Tower, knowing that she can do nothing to help her people. She can see her father and his warriors scurry around like ants far below, herding the Argaë into the towers until dense clouds of smoke obscure her view.

I have seen this before, Eireis remembers. And I was told that one would come…. Da-ni-el! She must awake from sleep to find him. But how to break free from the crystal now that Whiteday has come?

* * *

"Alright, lad, that's enough," Michael said. "We don't want to get too close to the shed. That should do anyway."

Although there were still quite a few canes left standing, the ground had been cleared enough for the next stage of the operation. Norbert extinguished the flamethrower regretfully.

"Now for the roots!" Michael said clapping his hands. "Fetch the rotovator, there's a good lad." He rolled himself another cigarette.

* * *

The fires of the Citadel had burned themselves out. Thousands had died in the fires but miraculously many more had survived in the underground passages and caverns deep below the ground. The Archon walks among his subjects estimating the damage and the number of casualties.

"Take what stores you have a go down into the caverns," he orders. "There is nothing to be salvaged from the ruins now."

* * *

From her vantage point, Eireis sees the rest of the evacuation underground. The Archon has sent soldiers into the Citadel and they collect the few survivors who have somehow managed to escape the flames.

A sudden roar suddenly makes her look up over the walls towards the plain. A Column of soil and rocks fountains high into the air as the earth is gouged open by some invisible force. The earth splits open with a terrible groan, and the crack propagates itself along the ground towards the Citadel. When the fault line reaches the badly charred and damaged walls, they explode into fragments and dust. The chasm continues deep into the city, destroying everything in its path.

* * *

Michael Meek was enjoying himself. Normally he left all the heavy work to Norbert, but he was having fun ploughing up the remainder of the briar. Anyway, the boy would probably veer off course and hit the wall or end up in the pond, he thought. The ground was heavy clay but, sheltered by the mass of the briar, it had remained fairly dry, so it was turning over quite nicely. There would have been no chance of doing this if it had been waterlogged.

Norbert followed behind with a fork and a wheelbarrow picking up the thick clusters of roots. Sometimes when they were already severed from their attached networks of rootlets, the big roots came out easily, but at others, Norbert had to use all his weight on the fork to rip them out of the ground. The roots resisted and then cracked and ripped, showing their succulent, white sap-rich hearts.

* * *

All around the Citadel the ground erupts, disgorging thousands of screaming, terrified Argaë from the protection of their underground shelters. There is no mercy this time. They are flung high into the air and ripped limb from limb by merciless invisible hands. Eireis witnesses the utter destruction of her home and the death of everyone she has ever known.

"Da-ni-el!" She screams at the Citadel is torn apart. The Archon's Tower, the last to stand, explodes, and Eireis is hurled headlong towards the churning ground.

She holds out her fists as if she were intending to strike earth with them. A split-second before the dreaming Eireis hits the ground, she wakes up with a start. She's lying on the floor of the cavern covered in the shards of her shattered sarcophagus. She is frozen to the bone and has difficulty standing up, but she struggles to her feet and begins the slow painful climb to the surface.

* * *

Michael Meek turned off the rotovator's engine and surveyed the results of his handiwork. Norbert was still struggling with a few of the thickest roots, but for the most part, the briar, nettles and other weeds would not be coming back in a hurry. Weeds always came back, he knew, as seeds carried into the gardens by birds and the wind, but for the next growing season, at least, there wouldn't be too many. All that was left to do was restore the central path and mark out the raised vegetable beds that Dan had requested.

"Good bit of work, Norbert," Michael said. "Let's have a cuppa."

Caroline looked out of the kitchen window as she filled up the kettle.

"They're finished," she said to Dan senior who had just come downstairs. "Look you can see right to the back wall. Seems a shame about the blackberries," she said.

"Plenty more in the woods," he replied, but he, too, felt uneasy about the destruction of the briar, though for the life of him he couldn't understand why.

–19–

The Lady Rosacea

Daniel's slow climb to the surface hasn't been enlivened by the merest glimmer of hope. He's at a loss at what to do next. He examines Eireis's gift again, wondering whether he should use it now, but thinks better of it and tucks it back under his cloak. He scans the gloomy, monochrome landscape. The sky, once so full of activity, is almost empty now, but from time to time, he spots the lights of a craft following its emerald path to the ground. Some of the tribes of the kingdom are still awake, digging their Whiteday shelters, but they are so engrossed by their preparations that they ignore him as he walks past.

He reaches one of the villages that he remembers seeing when Eireis had taken him to the battlements of the Citadel to show him the Green Kingdom for the first time. The houses were ramshackle and built in an absurd mixture of styles. Even now, when the village is mostly in ruins, he can see how strange the houses were when they were intact: stunted towers, domes, and gabled roofs, all assembled with no apparent plan or design. A solitary light burns on the ground floor of one of the houses. He approaches and knocks at the door.

"Who is it that walks in the failing Greenday light?" a cracked voice says from inside.

"I'm cold and lost. May I come in?" he pleads.

"Enter stranger. Friend or foe, there's little left here for you to take."

Daniel pushes open the door. Sitting inside beside a candle is an old woman. She wears a dress that must have once been very fine indeed – a creation made of layers of taffeta and lace – a kind of flowing ballgown. She wears a tiara on her white hair, though Daniel notices that most of the gems are lost, leaving the outline of the metal armature.

"Come closer, stranger," she says. "I cannot see very clearly now."

He walks into the small circle of candlelight.

"An Argaë by your clothes, but no Argaë walks now, they all sleep in their underground caverns." And then she sees his blue eyes. "A wonder…" she wheezes. But there is no fear in her voice.

"My name is Daniel," he says.

"Da-ni-el," she says, mouthing the unfamiliar syllables. "I am the Lady Rosacea," she says inclining her head in greeting.

Daniel remembers his grandfather's roses. He was so proud of them. Roses of every hue and size – shrub, dwarf, climbing – some with gigantic flowers with silky petals, others less showy but with overpowering musky scents. Dan senior had explained the mysteries of grafting one stock onto another, so that one type of rose carried the blooms of another, of the "royal" hybrid teas, the queens among roses. There were a few rosebushes left in the garden, he remembers. Poor leggy things, choked by the weeds.

"We once ruled supreme here in the Green Kingdom," she says sadly. "The Unseen Ones cared for us and protected us from our enemies, but no more".

"Why are you not getting ready to sleep?" he asks.

"I am ready for that sleep that never ends," she replies. I have no strength left to go down into the earth, no children to succeed me, no voice left to call to the Pool of Life."

* * *

Once the briar had been cleared, a space as large again as the lawn of the garden had been opened up, with a small pond, its brackish water choked with half-burnt weeds and briar canes, the old beehive, now long deserted and in ruins and the shed leaning precariously on the back wall, the fruit cage and vegetable beds had vanished altogether, chewed up by the metal jaws of the rotovator. Caroline was delighted with the extra space. Wait until Daniel sees this, she thought to herself.

"We can restore the pond, and the shed needs a lot work," Dan senior said appraising the damage.

"Whatever you think best," she said, only half-listening to his advice about, the shed, fruit cage and raised vegetable beds. "We could plant some strawberries, currants and raspberries," he said. "They'd make up for losing the blackberries."

Caroline eyed the old hive suspiciously as if it might suddenly come back to life. She'd been stung as a little girl. Although she'd never consulted a doctor to check if she'd developed an allergy, she'd convinced herself that she was allergic to bee stings, and that she'd probably die if she were ever stung again. She never had been, so she didn't actually know, but every time she saw anything that looked like a bee or wasp, she panicked and ran indoors.

"We need the bees," Dan senior said, almost as if he were sensing her discomfort as he began to dismantle the hive to see what, if any of it, could be salvaged. "They ensure the plants are pollinated, and that we get fruit and seeds every year. And there's the honey, of course. Nothing like homemade honey."

Caroline looked dubious. "Well, with the little one on the way..." she began.

"Never known a bee to attack unless it was provoked," he said. "Wasps, on the other hand, wasps is a different matter." Then changing the subject, he said pointing at the pond, "We'll need to fence that off for when she can crawl."

Caroline looked blankly at the pond. She'd never seen it as a threat. Adults could just about get their feet wet in it. But he was right. For a baby, it would a death trap. She was about to say something about the risk but thought better of it. I should learn to be braver, she thought. Not to worry so much. Her anxiety hadn't saved Daniel. On the contrary, she thought, if she'd let him run around more, he might not have been so clumsy.

"You're right," she began. "Homemade honey would be a treat."

* * *

"I could help you," Daniel says.

"Thank you, but I am beyond all help," the Lady Rosacea replies. "I will not live to see another Greenday. But what of you, Da-ni-el? You cannot stay here."

"I know," Daniel replies hanging his head. "But where can I go?"

"There are some who may yet help you," she says. "Go to the Great Kings."

Daniel recalls the formidable fortresses that he had seen from the glider.

"They are the mightiest among the tribes of the Green Kingdom," she explains. "They live for untold Greendays and Whitedays, with no fear of the perils of Whiteday and immune to the power of most of the Unseen Ones."

The old lady falls quiet, turns away and no longer seems to see and hear him. She is lost in a private world of past glories. Daniels stands up and, as quietly as he can, shuts the door behind him.

As he leaves the Lady Rosacea's ruined house, Daniel heads in the direction of the closest of the fortresses of the Great Kings. The Argaë's attitude to them, he remembers, was a mixture of fear and awe.

Even if they can help him, would those terrible beings want to? he wonders. He's a stranger in the Green Kingdom, and most of its inhabitants seemed to consider him to be an enemy and a threat. Looking at the sad houses of the village, he begins to understand why. We did this, he thinks. We took healthy, wild plants and changed them into these things for own amusement. What right did we have to interfere? He thinks of a favourite topic for his parents' arguments: GM crops and gene editing. His father was all for, his mother dead against. Daniel begins to wonder if his coming to the Green Kingdom was really a random accident. Was he brought here by someone or something? Maybe the Great Kings would know the answer.

– 20 –

The Great King

The sky is darker now and the wind blows ever colder. Daniel wraps the Argaë cloak around himself but its open weave was never intended to ward off the icy Whiteday chill. In the far distance, he can see the fortresses of the Great Kings. They stand in a jagged line on the horizon like an army of silent sentinels guarding the boundaries of the Green Kingdom. It's only when he approaches the gates of the first fortress that Daniel can appreciate its size. From a distance, there was no way of telling its scale, because there was nothing nearby to compare it to. No other tribes of the Green Kingdom build their homes in the shadow of the fortresses of the Great Kings, Eireis had told him, because they take all light and water for themselves.

    The fortress towers one hundred feet or more above him, with massive double doors that appear to be made of polished black stone etched with intricate silver geometric designs. Daniel stares up at the battlements. What you are here is not what you are in my world, he thinks. He looks hard at the fortress. For a moment the outline of the castle is superimposed with that of a tree – its black winter branches bare of leaves. A tree! He realises with glee, you're a tree.

But in the Green Kingdom, trees are huge, awesome beings, much larger than all the other plants. In his own world, his mother is always warning him not to climb them, while his father secretly wants him to.

He stands in front of the gigantic gates, unsure about what to do next. There is no obvious way in, nor is there even a means of making himself known to the inhabitants inside the fortress.

* * *

Much to Dan senior's surprise, Caroline had agreed to accompany him and Jeff to Mr Lachlan's cottage to see about getting some bees for the new hive they'd made for the back garden. Mr Lachlan had worked with Dan senior on the railways, until he, too, had retired. Now he lived in a cottage in the country with his bees. Mr Lachlan was called Bill, but to everyone he knew, he'd always been Mr Lachlan. Even Dan senior, who'd worked with him for thirty years, called him *Mister* Lachlan.

It was a fine late autumn day, and though there was still a little activity around the hives, with no more pollen or nectar to collect, the bees were getting ready for the winter. Mr Lachlan had already collected the honey he was going to take from each hive and replaced it with sugar solution to make sure the bees wouldn't go hungry.

Although she was still anxious around the bees, she couldn't help liking Mr Lachlan, who was big and jolly, and fussed about her, constantly steering her to chairs, as if a pregnant woman couldn't walk more than five steps before exhaustion got the better of her. She was, she had to admit, the size of a house. Daniel had been a big baby, but his sister was going to be even bigger.

An ancient horse chestnut dominated the garden. It was a tall and stately and had so far escaped the fungal disease that had disfigured so many of the conker trees in the area. The disease was caused by a fungus that had suddenly appeared from nowhere, and she was sure in that it was another disaster caused by climate change, which had seen new pests and diseases take advantage of the warming climate to extend their range northwards. She sat in a chair by the cottage's open back door and watched the two older men inspect the hives. Jeff, she noticed, kept his distance, while Dan senior and Mr Lachlan, peered into the hives unconcerned by the occasional sentinel bee who flew up to investigate them.

She stood up and walked over to the horse chestnut. Conkers littered the ground where they'd fallen, their green husks split open, revealing the shiny brown seeds within. They were the colour of rich, dark chocolate, she used to think when she was a little girl. She was feeling a little tired, so she rested her hand on the trunk to catch her breath. It was then that she noticed the bee for the first time. It was a few inches from her hand, a bee was just sitting on the trunk – a tiny yellow-and-black jewel against the mottled brown of the bark. The insect walked slowly towards her fingers, stopped, and looked up at her.

For the first time since she'd been stung, Caroline wasn't worried by the insect. The vast majority of bees are infertile females whose lives are spent serving their queen, she remembered Dan senior telling her. They do all the work: look after the brood, collect the pollen and nectar, make the honey, tidy up, and keep the hive safe – she suddenly felt a sisterly sympathy for the hardworking bee. I bet no one thanks you either, she thought.

The bee climbed onto her hand and began to dance, alternately raising its head and its abdomen, circling one way, then another. Caroline could feel the pattern of the tiny dancing feet on her skin. She suddenly had the absurd thought that the bee was trying to tell her something.

"Darling, are you alright?" Jeff asked, striding towards her, with the two older men in tow.

Caroline turned to look at him. "I'm fine," she replied. "I was just...." She looked back at her hand but the bee had flown off and was nowhere to be seen.

"Anything wrong?" Mr Lachlan asked concerned. "Shall I bring a chair?"

"Oh, no, Mr Lachlan. I'm fine. really. I was just admiring your conker tree."

Jeff looked over to his father. "Dad was wondering... that is, I was wondering if we could..." he began but he was having difficulty finding the most tactful way of asking Caroline if Dan, senior could keep bees again.

"It'd be nice to have some homemade honey," she said simply, and she turned and started to walk back towards the cottage.

Dan senior beamed at her, and Jeff stared open-mouthed because he hadn't been privy to her change of heart about bees.

"Getting a bit chilly," Mr Lachlan said. "Let's go indoors and have some tea. I've got some teacakes in special – a treat with honey."

* * *

"Anyone there?" Daniel calls out at the top of his voice, but his words are lost among the towering ramparts. He bangs on the doors with his fists but barely manages to make a sound. He hunts around for something hard with which he can strike the door, but there's not even a rock on the ground. It's as if it's been swept clean. He feels on his belt for his dagger, but the sheath is empty. He must have lost it sometime after leaving the Citadel in the skyboat landing. Next to it, tucked into the belt, is the pouch containing Eireis's mysterious gift. He lets the pouch float up on the cord that draws it closed. Lighter than air, he reasons. Maybe he can use it to fly over the fortress's walls. But the pouch is much too small to bear his weight. Maybe he has to release the contents into the air or say a magic word. He studies it more closely. The opening is sealed by a small wooden stopper, like those on the Argaë waterskins he drank from in the Citadel. Maybe he is supposed to "drink" the contents. Wake up, Daniel! he scolds himself. This isn't a Harry Potter or Alice in Wonderland magic potion!

He carefully takes out the stopper and quickly covers the opening with his lips to prevent the contents from escaping. Warm air rushes into his mouth; it tastes of pastures immediately after the rain, and of warm summer days, of forests in winter – each mouthful seems to evoke some new sensory memory. Once he has swallowed the last of the contents, he waits for something to happen. Will he be able to fly? But his feet remain stubbornly attached to the ground. He strikes the door experimentally, half-expecting his fist to go through the polished surface, but the material is just as unyielding as before.

He opens his mouth and sighs. A howling wind issues from him mouth. He clamps his mouth shut. That's strange, he thinks.

He turns to face the fortress and shouts, "I come to see the Great Kings!" His voice amplified by the contents of the pouch is so loud that it shakes the foundations of the fortress. Stones are dislodged from the walls and rain down around him, forcing him to jump back to avoid being crushed. Then everything falls quiet. He breathes out carefully but whatever power he had possessed is now gone.

In the distance he can hear a clanking noise, as if some ancient machinery had been set in motion. The great double doors swing open slowly and ponderously, revealing only darkness within. After a moment's hesitation, Daniel walks in. He senses that he is in an enormous space. He can make out great dark shapes ahead, but there isn't enough light to see what these might be.

Straight ahead, a dim halo of light appears over one of the great shapes. It is a giant many times Daniel's height sitting on a stone throne. The figure wears a crown and a long flowing gown. His face is lined with age, and his eyes are almost shut, as if he were just awakening from a deep sleep.

"Who stands in the hall of King Quercus?" a voice asks, echoing in the cavernous space, but at the same time, it seems cracked and weak for all its power. "You come in the garb of the Argaë, but you are no Argaë, as none of that tribe would ever dare come into our presence."

"I am Daniel," he manages to reply. I hope the great king is like the BFG, he thinks.

"Come closer, Da-ni-el," the king says. "Let me look at you."

Shaking from the cold as much as from fear, Daniel walks to the base of the throne. Now that he is close by, he can see that the King's clothes are musty and covered with mould, and his skin is pitted and wrinkled like the bark of an ancient tree. The king breathes slowly and heavily. He peers at Daniel through eyes weakened by age and disease.

"You are not of the Green Kingdom!" the king wheezes. "I can see it by your eyes. You are a stranger, a destroyer! Be gone, foul creature!" the king orders weakly.

Surprised by this turn of events, it is Daniel who feels obliged to speak out. "Please," he begins. "I mean you no harm. I've come to ask for your help."

"My help?" the king says, but his voice is still suspicious. "I never thought I would ever meet a creature such as you," he says. "How did you come to be in the Green Kingdom?"

Daniel does his best to explain his arrival in the Green Kingdom, but his explanation makes little sense even to him. The events have become confused in his own mind. "I am trapped here," he says finally. "And I need to find a way home before the Lethe returns."

The king seems to give the matter some thought then says, "I can tell you only what I know of your kingdom. In the dawn of time," he begins, "there was but one kingdom, the White Kingdom, and this remained so for ages untold. Then from the White Kingdom there emerged two new kingdoms: the Green Kingdom, in which you now stand, and your own, the Red Kingdom. New tribes appeared unlike any that had previously existed, and as they grew and multiplied, the kingdoms were soon divided. With each passing age, the contact between the two kingdoms became more difficult until the bridges between them were broken altogether. The ancient tribes that had spanned both kingdoms vanished, and the creatures of the Red Kingdom – the Unseen Ones, as we call them – both wondrous and terrible, became shadows that only a few of the most gifted among our kind can contact during the time of Calling. But even then, for ages uncountable, there existed a balance between the kingdoms."

The king falls silent, exhausted by the effort of speaking for so long. Finally, he goes on, "Ages more passed and the two kingdoms, though separate, continued to live in harmony. But this, too, was not to last. Once the Green Kingdom had been the realm of Great Kings in vast numbers, but soon a great storm descended upon us, and millions of my kind perished, victims of the Red Kingdom, which has grown so greatly that it threatens the very existence of the Green Kingdom. In places, the land is barren, and all but the hardiest tribes have perished and been forced to flee. If things continue in this manner, we shall all be destroyed. But that will not be all, for we know that one kingdom cannot survive alone, and the destruction of one will mean the destruction of the other.

"I don't understand how you came to be amongst us," the king says. "But I believe that it is no mere an accident. You must return to the Red Kingdom and restore the balance between the two realms."

"Me?" It is Daniel's turn to be shocked. He had come here as a supplicant in search of help. "What can I do? I do not have power in my world. I am no great king or a warrior," he says.

"Great kings and warriors are not born but often made by chance or necessity," the king replies wearily, his eyes half-closed from exhaustion.

"But I do not even know how to return to the Red Kingdom," Daniel says miserably.

"Do not despair," the king says kindly, his voice faltering to a whisper. "You came through a gateway between the kingdoms once, so it must be possible for you to return. But," he adds more sternly. "Do not delay here much longer, as the coming of Whiteday is upon us, and if the Lethe touches you, you will certainly die." Almost as a second thought, he says. "Seek out your own kind, the Unseen Ones that visit us. They will hold the key to your safe return… seek out the Unseen Ones…"

The ghostly halo fades, as the king sinks back into sleep. Daniel hears the machinery of the doors begin to close. He runs back the way he came, crossing the giant threshold just before the gates slam shut.

A Forgotten Enemy

During the little time Daniel spent with the king, the sky has grown darker and the wind now blows icy cold. It won't be long before the darkness returns, he thinks. The plain is deserted now: the cities, encampments, villages and towns crumble into ruin. All he hears is the sound of decay and destruction. And soon, he knows, the Lethe will return to smother the ground in ice and snow to complete the year's cycle. The Green Kingdom will sleep during the coming Whiteday, the winter of his world, and reawaken next Greenday, his world's spring, some three months away. He knows that he won't be able survive for that long on his own.

Where should I go? he asks himself. The king told him seek the Unseen Ones, but how is he supposed to find them? He suddenly thinks that Eireis's gift might have been a way of getting in touch with the Unseen Ones, but now he's wasted it.

His mood becomes more desperate than before, and with nowhere else to go, he decides to return to the cavern beneath the new citadel where he'd left Eireis. He knows that there he will be safe from the Lethe, at least, and even if he cannot sleep in a sarcophagus, he will find warmth underground. In the

Citadel, he'd been sustained by their food, and when he had first met Eireis, he remembers, she'd given him food from the Argaë's Whiteday stores. He knows the Argaë have brought supplies with them and stored them in the tunnels leading down to the cavern. Maybe with those, he could make it through to the next Greenday.

He heads back the way he came, but in the growing darkness, he's lost the few landmarks that have guided him until now. He estimates that he has walked as far as he did when he left, but he still doesn't see the entrance to the cavern marked by the wicker dome and palisade. He's about to give up when he sees a familiar rounded shape in the gloom. He runs towards it.

He reaches it quickly but realises immediately that it's not the dome that he'd left. Tools and supplies lie abandoned around the wellhead. This is another Argaë landing site, but not one as fortunate as his own. He peers down into the well and can just make out the top of a ladder. He tests the rope that descends into the darkness. The post to which it's attached creaks ominously as it takes the strain, but it holds as he climbs down to the ledge. The ladder is intact and leads down into an unlit tunnel. More tools and supplies lie scattered, abandoned by the Argaë. But what threat could make them abandon their precious supplies and tools?

A distant tremor makes the tunnel shake, showering him with dust. Unseen Ones, he thinks. But these are probably not the beautiful creatures that

Eireis had summoned during the Calling, nor even the terrifying cloud beasts, one of which had swallowed them whole. He remembers the horrible monsters he'd seen depicted on the walls of the Tower of the Lore. He follows the tunnels down to the entrance of the crystal cavern, which is lit by the faint glow of the crystals. At first, he thinks that the Argaë are asleep and that all is well, but as he begins to climb down the steep staircase, he sees that many of the crystals have been knocked over.

He has reached the outer ring of crystals but not one is left standing or intact. They have been smashed open. Every single sarcophagus is empty, but some contain a sign of their owner's presence: a tool, an item of clothing, a weapon. He feels a breeze on his face in what should be a closed space. He turns. Something has gouged a dozen gigantic holes in the walls and ceiling of the cavern.

"Bore worms," says a voice from behind him. Daniel wheels around. Margrave, his old enemy, is standing leaning on his staff. He is injured. His forehead is smeared with dried blood from a gash on his temple. "They attacked the cavern, and the fools summoned the Pool of Life to save themselves, thinking they would be safe in the sarcophagi. But the worms can only see the crystals. They are blind to all else. They sealed themselves into their own coffins!"

"And you let them do it although you knew it would mean their deaths?" Daniel asks.

"Of course. They showed me no respect. They all deserved to die!" Margrave screams. He begins to laugh a low evil cackle. "As you shall soon, stranger! Devoured by your own foul kind!"

"Your magic can't hurt me, Margrave. You tried once, remember," Daniel spits out. "Goodbye, Margrave, I leave you to whatever fate has in store for you."

But before Daniel has a chance to catch his breath, Margrave raises his staff and a stream of blue flame races towards the tunnels made by the worms. At the same moment, he utters the same high-pitched note Eireis had sung out when calling to the Pool of Life. Margrave lunges forwards dropping his staff and grabs hold of Daniel.

The Pool of Life rises into the form of Margrave and extends its watery arms around the struggling pair. Daniel knows that he cannot be enclosed in a crystal, but it will certainly encase Margrave. The water bounces over Daniel's skin but solidifies before it touches the ground. But wherever it touches Margrave, it begins to form the base of a sarcophagus.

A terrifying roar makes both of them freeze. A giant worm, its skin covered in iridescent brown-black scales bursts into the cavern from one of the holes that it or others of its kind have gouged in the wall. It has no eyes that Daniel can see, but it turns towards the area where the empty crystals lie all around them. It sees the crystals with some sense other than sight.

The worm opens it giant maw, and a dozen tentacles tipped with claw-like scales dart out. They lift one of the empty sarcophagi and probe its interior. Discovering it empty, the worm casts it aside. Margrave calls out trying to imitate the worm's roar. It rears its head towards them. But the effort of fighting Daniel, while he controls the pool and summons the worm, is too much for the loremaster. Daniel manages to break free from his grasp and jumps to the side. In seconds the sarcophagus closes over Margrave's head.

The worm, sensing a new prey, leaps forwards onto Margrave's newly formed sarcophagus. The tentacles grab it and wrenching it from the floor and lifting into the air. Inside a terrified Margrave smashes at the crystal with his fists trying vainly to break it open. Two of the clawed tentacles, their tips razor sharp, slice the top of the crystal open, while the others reach into the interior to seize the struggling, screaming Margrave. The tentacles pull the body into the gaping mouth of the worm, which snaps shut. A terrible crunching of bones is followed by the leathery sounds of the worm swallowing its prey. Daniel dares not breathe, lest the noise alert the monster to his presence. Satisfied that there is no more food to be had, the worm slowly turns and leaves the cavern by the way it came. The silence returns, but there is no peace here, only desolation and death. Daniel runs from the place, not stopping until he reaches the relative safety of the surface.

* * *

Dan senior was tending to the hive in the back garden. It was as far back from the house as possible in deference to Caroline, against the back wall, which also sheltered it from the wind. Although it was sunny, the late-autumn air was already chilly. Mr Lachlan had decided to downsize, and he had given Dan senior one of his hives. It wasn't usual to move bees so late in the year. But at least it would disturb them as little as possible to move them then rather than in the spring. There was no pollen or nectar to gather, and the hive was mostly ticking over.

Caroline had made Dan senior and herself a cup of tea and took it out to him with a plate of biscuits. She kept out of the back garden, just by the ivy-covered arch, and called out to him.

"I should have thought they'd be all asleep by now," Caroline said from a safe distance. "No flowers left to feed off."

"Oh, they don't sleep through the winter," he corrected her. "Many of the workers die, but the ones who live stay awake to tend to the queen and the brood. I was just checking for pests. Even at this time of year, a wasp can sneak in and make a mess. And you always have to keep an eye out for disease."

Like most city-dwellers, Caroline was vaguely aware of the savage nature of life inside a hive, and like most, she preferred not to think that the honey she spread over her toast in the morning had been produced thanks to the exploitation of others, even if they were insects. A bee flew past Caroline heading towards house. She studied its slow erratic flight.

"I've never known them to be so active this late in the year," Dan senior said. "It's almost as they're looking for something," he added as another squadron of four bees flew out of the hive entrance.

As they chatted and drank their tea, neither of them noticed the old queen bee emerge from the hive. She was not a great flier, having not flown since her coronation flight with the drones. She half-flew, half-glided onto Dan jacket and made his way into the breast pocket of the jacket that he always wore even when he was at home. She settled in the folds of the neatly pressed handkerchief that he always carried but never ever used. He had another in his trouser pocket.

"Look at the time," Caroline said looking at her watch. "I should be getting ready to go to the hospital. Do you want to come?" she asked.

"Yes, let me get my coat," he replied. He went back into the back garden to where he had left his jacket hung up on a branch near the hive. The bees were still flying about. "What's got into you?" he said under his breath.

He slipped the jacket on and went to join his daughter-in-law for the short drive to the hospital.

* * *

The Greenday sun is almost extinguished now. It's just the faintest of glows on the distant horizon. Ice crystals swirl in the wind, harbingers the deep freeze that will soon envelop the Green Kingdom. He walks in the direction of what he hopes is the Argaë palisade where he left Eireis, but he's afraid that he's now completely lost.

No! It will not end this way, he reproaches himself. I won't give up! Did Harry Potter give up and feel sorry for himself when Voldemort was winning? Did Alice sit down and cry when she was in trouble with the Queen of Hearts? No, they fought on. Shame they're imaginary…. But he picks up the pace, and heads towards any shape he can still see on the plain. He comes to several fences and palisades, but none of them are of Argaë construction. He begins to run blindly.

"Da-ni-el! Stop! Da-ni-el!" Eireis shouts.

The Queen of the Hive

"Da-ni-el!" Eireis calls out again.

In Daniel's headlong rush, he's run straight past the dome and palisade he was searching for. Eireis is standing by the entrance to the dome, her cloak tightly wrapped around her, her face pallid and drawn.

"What are you doing here? You shouldn't be outside now," he says, but she's so weak that she staggers and almost falls. He catches her in his arms and feels how cold she is even though both their cloaks. Slowly, she seems to revive. It's as if he were somehow transferring heat from his body to hers. A little colour returns to her face, and she stops shivering.

"Let's get out of the wind," he says, leading her back under the dome. "Why did you come up to the surface? You should have stayed asleep."

"I could not leave you out here alone, Da-ni-el," she replies. "Leaving my sarcophagus at will is one power that only I and a few of the loremasters possess among the Argaë."

"Yes, I know," Daniel replies. He tells her of his meeting with Margrave in the other cavern, and of the loremaster's fate.

"How horrible!" she says. "You saw the bore worms?" He nodded. "To us, like all Unseen Ones, they are invisible – their presence sensed but they themselves are never seen. You are no longer fully this kingdom, Da-ni-el."

Daniel realises what she means. He often sees two superimposed images when he looks at something: the Lady Rosacea and a flowering rose, the Great King and a tree, but he's also changed physically. So late in Greenday, he should feel chilled to the bone and weak like the other inhabitants of the Green Kingdom, but although he does feel cold, he's not as weak as Eireis. A lot of it is in his head, he realises. If he concentrates, he feels warmth, as if his body were somewhere else – somewhere much warmer than the Green Kingdom. And as long as Eireis stays near him, she, too, seems to be immune from the chill of Whiteday.

He tells her of his visit to the Lady Rosacea and tries to explain that she is a "flower," a hybrid product of selective breeding and grafting by the gardeners of his world.

"You mean, your kind have the power to alter the tribes in the Green Kingdom?" she asks aghast.

"Yes, I think we can," he replies. "But I'm not sure we always do it well or wisely." He thinks of the Lady Rosacea and the other domesticated plants that cannot thrive without the care of humans, and he also wonders about the gene-edited and -modified crops his parents are always arguing about. What will happen to the Green Kingdom if our experiments go wrong? The Green Kingdom is ancient – much older than the Red Kingdom. But humans, his mother says, are interfering with the building blocks of life. He continues his story and tells her of his visit to the Great King, and of what they know of the origins of the two kingdoms.

"I begin to understand," she says. "I can piece this together with the things I know from Argaë Lore. You and the Invisible Ones are of the same Red Kingdom that we can neither see nor feel. How you came to be here, I cannot say, but I might still be able to help you get back. It's a thing that has never been done before in the long history of the Argaë, but I must try to rebuild the bridge with the Red Kingdom that was broken."

"How will you do that?" he asks.

"I will use my power to call the Unseen Ones."

"But are you sure about what kind of Unseen Ones you'll call?" Daniel asks, imagining the monsters that might come instead of the benign Unseen Ones that had visited the Citadel during the Calling.

"Come," she says pointing to the base of a nearby tower. The building is empty and dark, long since stripped and abandoned by its builders who have moved to their underground Whiteday quarters. The tower, sturdily built, however, is mostly intact. The doorway is low, because its builders are of lower stature than the Argaë, and the markings and reliefs on its walls are in a completely different style than the ones Daniel was used to seeing in the Citadel.

"This is a Chadri tower," she explains. "Help me clear the entrance."

Daniel hauls pieces of fallen timber and masonry from the ruined gateway to create a narrow opening. But the narrow spiral staircase within is mostly unobstructed and seems solid enough. They climb half a dozen floors and emerge onto an open-air platform halfway up the tower. They look up to the summit from which a great crown of spine-like projections juts out at right angles from the walls. From there they climb an external staircase wrapped around the central core of the tower. The upper reaches of the tower are badly damaged, and several of the steps sag and creak ominously under their weight.

They're almost at the top when a violent gust of wind shakes loose one of the giant spines above them. It crashes down towards them. They just have time enough to flatten themselves against the wall to avoid being knocked off the staircase. The spine smashes into the wall and bounces into the stairs below, sheering several cleanly off and leaving a gap too big to jump.

"We're trapped!" Daniel says.

"Quick!" says Eireis, "before another comes down!"

They run up to the top of a tower, which is a broad platform just above the spines. The upper part of the building sways alarmingly in the wind; timbers groan under their feet as another two spines snaps off, destroying more of the staircase and the tower below.

I've condemned her to death, Daniel thinks horrified. But Eireis is already climbing to the highest part of the tower.

"Help me, Da-ni-el." He hurries after her, remembering that it is only when she is near him that he can lend her his warmth and strength. She stands on the very edge of the crumbling battlements.

* * *

Caroline and Dan senior went into Daniel's hospital room. Dan senior shut the door, trying not to make a sound. He'd never quite gotten used the idea that in his comatose state his grandson couldn't be disturbed by the noises his visitors made. Caroline turned on the TV, sat down by the bed and took out her knitting. Dan senior sat down in the chair on the other side of Daniel's bedside and began to read his paper. The queen emerged from his pocket and crawled unnoticed down his jacket and along his trouser leg until she was only a few inches from Daniel's bed. She launched herself across the gap between Dan senior's knee and the bed and hid under the sheets.

* * *

Daniel stands behind Eireis, holding her in his arms, both to keep her from falling and to keep her warm and awake. She begins to intone the same complex, clear, wordless chant that he'd heard before in the Citadel during the Calling, but in the gathering darkness there seems to be something wrong with their harmonics. The call has lost some of the purity and joyfulness he remembers. Its echoes trail off, harsh and dissonant, as if they were grating on the freezing Whiteday air. Eireis falls quiet and for a moment, and the world, too, becomes completely still. She looks towards the horizon where the sun is no brighter than the faintest star in the night sky.

A sudden gust of wind catches her and throws her off balance. She falls forwards, almost pulling them both off the tower. He braces himself with his feet until he's steady enough to pull them both back. She looks at him in shock. But another gust shakes the whole tower. Tortured groans signal the collapse of columns and supports below them. The tower sways violently from side to side.

But still the horizon is empty. Has it been all in vain? Are they to meet their end here and now, so that no one will ever know of his adventures in the Green Kingdom?

A high-pitched buzzing makes them both look up. Something is materialising directly above them. It looks like an inverted whirlpool opening up in the air. With a terrible and final crashing sound, the Chadri tower begins to collapse. Floors crash into one another, like the closing of a giant concertina.

Daniel holds on to Eireis, hoping that his invulnerability will protect her too. But as the tower falls away, they remain motionless, suspended in the air, supported by an invisible force. The buzzing gets louder. There is a battle going on between the force of gravity pulling them downwards and the force exerted by the buzzing vortex above them. For a moment, it seems that gravity is going to win, sending them plummeting into the twisted wreckage of the tower, but then infinitely slowly, they begin to rise.

They're carried up until they are inside the vortex, which they now see is made up of hundreds of winged shapes flying in a spiral that is lost in the heights far above, drawing them ever upwards. The air has suddenly become warm. Wordlessly, the Unseen Ones welcome them and tell them that they come at the behest of their queen to take them to her realm.

The displacement stops suddenly and they are left standing in a vast circular hall supported by massive stone pillars. Between each pillar is an arch-shaped opening. Daniel looks up but he cannot see a ceiling, only floor after floor going up into infinity.

"Welcome to my realm," says a voice that sounds both close by and far away. Indistinct shapes appear in each archway. Thousands upon thousands of figures look down on them, but neither Daniel nor Eireis is afraid. "Never has this happened in the entire history of the two kingdoms," the voice goes on.

The air in front of them thickens and swirls. Golden dust rises in columns, forming successions of patterns in the air that change too quickly for Daniel's eyes to register them. Gradually they settle as figures crystalise around them.

Iridescent beings stand next to a throne on which sits the queen.

Daniel can see two superimposed images: a woman, wearing a gold and black robe and a jewelled crown, attended by a court of richly attired ladies-in-waiting, and the shape of winged creatures with huge multifaceted eyes, six legs and a body striped with yellow and black bands.

"Welcome Caller of the Argaë," the queen says. "It is long ages since we last welcomed one of the Green Kingdom into the Hive. To you also, Da-ni-el of the Red Kingdom, welcome. You have crossed a bridge that none of your kind have ever dreamed of or seen. But now you must return to your home, because you cannot remain in the Green Kingdom through the coming Whiteday."

"Can you take me home?" Daniel asks the queen.

"You exist in both kingdoms at once. The physical part of you never left the Red Kingdom, but you spirit was allowed to exist in the Green Kingdom." She stands up. "Come with me," she says leading them to a nearby archway. It opens into a long tunnel at the end of which Daniel can see a bright light, but it is not the light of the Green Kingdom. The world beyond the opening is a chaos of swirling shapes and colours. Daniel becomes dizzy looking at it.

"The passage of time is different in the two kingdoms," the queen explains. "Close your eyes and look through mine."

Daniel closes his eyes but can still see. The maelstrom gradually slows.

"My eyes are not as yours, Da-ni-el," says the queen. "They are many facetted and produce many images at the same time. You must seek out the repeating patterns."

It's like looking at the patterns in a kaleidoscope, Daniel thinks. The same pattern is reflected hundreds of time. Gradually Daniel starts to make sense of the swirling shapes: trees, shrubs, individual leaves and branches, grass. This is a garden, his memory tells him – the garden of Greenacres. Looking through the ivy-covered arch, he can make is the main garden with its lawn and flowerbeds, and beyond them, the house itself. It looks gigantic through the queen's eyes, it towers over the garden like one of the fortresses of the Great Kings.

"I know this place," Daniel says. "This is my home."

Farewells

"I better get back. I've got the supper to do," Caroline said. "Are you coming, dad?"

"I'll stay here with the lad a bit longer," Dan senior replied looking up from his paper. "I'll take the bus home. Don't you worry about me. But will you be alright?"

"I may be the size of a house, dad, but I can still drive, push a shopping trolley, carry a shopping bag home and cook supper," she said laughing as she put her knitting into her bag. "I'll see you at home about seven".

To be honest, Dan senior was looking forwards to a couple of hours of peace and quiet. Not that he was ungrateful that his son and daughter-in-law had taken him in and given him a home (even if it was in his own house). But sometimes he missed living alone – even living alone in his room at the home – where he could shut the door and retire into a private world of memories. At home, there was Caroline during the day, forever fussing over him or asking him to help with something around the house or garden, and in the evening, it was Jeff's turn. It was as if the boy were trying to make up for twenty years of silence all in one go. He made a point of asking him for his opinion, invited him to go down to the pub, and discussed his career and future plans. It was nice, he thought to himself, but old people, he reflected, also needed a lot more time to themselves.

He got up to turn the television off. It was one of those idiot afternoon TV shows in which dysfunctional families paraded their sins for the enjoyment of the nation: infidelities, divorces, addictions, children born out of wedlock. There but for the grace of God go we, he said to himself.

The queen waited under the covers, acting as a link between the physical Daniel in the hospital bed and the one in the Green Kingdom. She knew that what she was doing was going to cost her her life, but she had left instructions to her daughters to raise two new queens in readiness for the next spring. One would take over, while the other would swarm.

* * *

"This is home," Daniel says recognizing the house and garden. He finally understands it all: who he is and who all the voices in his head are – his parents and his grandfather, who are real, and the fictional characters – Harry Potter, Hermione, Ron, Alice and Frodo – who are made up. He remembers what happened to him: the weekend-long row, his running into the garden, slipping on the wet stones of the path, falling and hitting his head. And then somehow, he had woken up in the Green Kingdom – not his body, he now knows, but just his spirit or soul, or whatever part of him this is. He looks at the garden and sees how different it looks from the way he remembers. The lawn and beds have been tidied up, and the archway to the back garden is clear of its thick curtain of ivy.

"Can we go there," Daniel says, indicating the back garden.

Two of the iridescent beings – two bees – lift him and Eireis higher into the air. They fly towards the back garden. Daniel finds it a lot easier to decipher the patterns that he can see through the queen's eyes. The ivy on the archway has been neatly clipped back. Daniel is struck dumb by what he sees. Instead of the towering briar that he'd expected to find – the Citadel of the Argaë – he sees a couple of raised vegetable beds, well-tended and -tilled, with not a weed in sight, a shed, a pond, a new fruit cage and a beehive.

"The Citadel is gone!" Eireis cries out in desolation. She sees mostly what exists in the Green Kingdom. To her eyes, where there should be the ruins of great towers and mighty ramparts, there is nothing left at all. As if the ground had been swept clean. There is no sign of life apart from the ever-present bulk of the fortresses of the Great Kings.

"Now I understand the great pain I felt, Da-ni-el. And what the Great King meant when he said he feared you and your kind. How can your tribe sweep away so much with so little care? What right do you have?" she says angrily.

"I'm sorry," is all Daniel can think to say. But now that he remembers, he knows that in the real world – his world – thing are very different. People don't imagine that plants could possibly have lives of their own, let alone thoughts, feelings or personalities – they probably don't think of plants as living beings at all, come to think of it. They can barely manage it with animals and other humans, he thinks sadly. But it's more complicated than that, too. To humans, the tribes he has met, the Argaë, the briars, the Urtikai, the nettles, and the Chadri, the thistles, are thought of as weeds to be ruthlessly uprooted and banished from gardens. They're fine in woodlands, but people pull them up in their gardens to allow other plants grow – the plants that they've decided aren't weeds. Or those they have changed to meet their specifications, like the hybrid roses – the sad, faded Lady Rosacea.

Daniel concentrates and looks at the garden through his Green Kingdom eyes. There must be life somewhere, even now.

* * *

Caroline arrived home with two heavy shopping bags. Maybe she should have accepted Dan senior's offer of help. As she filled the kettle to make herself a cup of tea, she looked out of the kitchen window. For some reason that she couldn't fathom, she had the feeling that Daniel was in the back garden right at this very moment. She scolded herself for being so silly. She'd just left him in a coma in his hospital bed. But the feeling was so strong that she put down the kettle, unlocked the back door and stepped out into the garden. It was chilly and already growing dark, but there was still just enough light to see by.

This is ridiculous, she thought. What am I doing? But she felt his presence so strongly that she couldn't help herself. She had to go to the back garden to check, no matter how ridiculous and pointless it seemed. She was glad that neither Jeff nor Dan senior were home. She reached the arch and stepped through. It was then that she saw the hive, or rather, what was on the hive. Hundreds of bees had left the safety and warmth of the interior and were crawling over the outside. The roof of the hive was a writhing mass of insects. The eeriest thing, Caroline remembered later, was that they had been completely silent. She had always thought of bees as buzzing noisily, but these were not making a sound.

Her fear of being stung was replaced by curiosity about what was going on. She'd learned a lot about bees since Dan senior had brought the new hive, and she knew that this wasn't usual. They can't possibly be swarming now, she thought. Surely, that must happen in the spring or summer when there was plenty of food of them. What she didn't know was that something that had never happened before had happened, because the queen had abandoned her colony to go to Daniel.

* * *

"Mum!" Daniel shouts. He can see the familiar figure of his mother – a giantess in the multifaceted bee's eyes – and also as she might appear to the Argaë, as a huge, blobby Unseen One, with no separate head or arms.

"The Unseen One cannot see you in this form, Da-ni-el," the voice of the queen says in his head, transmitted by telepathy through the worker bees that carry them.

* * *

Caroline studied the bees from a respectful distance, then having assured herself that, as she already knew, Daniel wasn't in the back garden, she turned and walked slowly back to the house. She made a mental note to ask Dan senior about what she'd seen.

* * *

Daniel watches his mother until she has walked back into the house and has shut and bolted the kitchen door behind her. She stares out of the kitchen window, silhouetted against the bright kitchen light, before turning and walking out of sight.

"Can we fly beyond the garden," Daniel asks the queen.

The bees fly higher, flying over the back garden. The garden wall looms up in front of them, as tall as any cliff Daniel has even seen. The bees are making straight for it at high speed. He is sure that they will crash into it, but just before they collide with it, they change course and fly vertically up the sheer face. Daniel is exhilarated – it's the best ride he's ever been on – much better than the rides he'd been to at the funfairs that he'd been to on the common on bank holidays.

After overtopping the wall, the bees plunge down the other side in a dizzying descent. They come to a sudden halt a few paces from the ground. It's almost dark in both the Red and Green Kingdoms. Only the warmth emanating from the bees is keeping Eireis awake.

At last, Daniel sees what he was looking for. "Look! Over there!" he calls out.

Just on the inside of the wall, a small green shoot has broken through the rich black loam strewn with fallen leaves. It's both a young shoot and the dome the Argaë had built after their flight in the skyboat.

He asks the bees to drop them just by the entrace, thanks them and sends them back to the hive. At once, he is back in the Green Kingdom. The ground is already dusted with snow, and ice crystals swirl through the air. The wicker dome is already frosted white. He looks around anxiously, expecting the Lethe to spring on them, but there's no sign of the deadly white mist.

So late in Greenday and away from the bees, Eireis seems to have almost no strength left. Even when he holds her, she's barely conscious. He has to carry her into the palisade. He finds a piece of rope abandoned by the builders and uses it to tie the unconscious Eireis to his back, so that he can carry her down the ladder to the first ledge and the tunnel that leads downward to warmth and safety.

As soon as he reaches the first tunnel, he picks up the pace, walking down the dark passages as fast as he dares, guided by the warmth that he feels coming up from the cavern below. Finally, he reaches his goal and is relieved to see that the sarcophagi are all intact. He carefully carries Eireis down to the edge of the Pool of Life.

He wonders what he should do now, but the water in the pool begins to bubble of its own accord. He watches as the water rises into a column that then solidifies into a human shape. He's amazed to see that it is his own.

"Da-ni-el..." his water double whispers. It's not exactly a voice, more of an approximation of his voice somehow constructed from watery sounds.

"Can you help me," Daniels asks the pool indicating the sleeping Eireis.

The water Daniel extends his arms and begins to spin slowly, sending out streamers of water from his fingers. The water passes straight through Daniel, leaving no sign of its passage. It reaches out to the body of Eireis, lifting her gently off the ground. It carries her to the vacant place of honour and sets her down on her feet. In moments, she is encased in the translucent blue-green sarcophagus. The water Daniel begins to subside back into the pool.

"Now you must return, Da-ni-el..." the water Daniel says. "Return to the Red Kingdom...." And with those words, it is gone.

Daniel is left alone. He walks up to Eireis's sarcophagus. "Goodbye," he says.

Awakening

Daniel climbs wearily up to the surface. The world he sees is a strange composite of the Green Kingdom and the garden at Greenacres. Superimposed over the snow-covered ruins of the Green Kingdom and the fortresses of the Great Kings are images of wilted stalks, bare earth and leafless trees. The garden wall rises straight ahead of him, at the same time low, worn and moss-covered brick and impossibly high, smooth polished black stone. Beyond it is the safety of home, if only he could reach it.

An intense cold has now descended over the Green Kingdom– as bad as it was when he'd first woken up there. It's not long before he hears the sound he's been dreading. The strange sighing voice of the Lethe: "Ssssssssllllllllllllleeeeeeeeeeeepppppppppppp!"

Daniel is looking up at the garden wall. He spins around and sees that the Lethe has cut off his every avenue of retreat. There is no escape into the underground and no tower to climb this time. The Lethe hesitates as it had done the first time it had encountered him. It's again puzzled – although Daniel doesn't understand how a mist can sense anything. Swirls of insubstantial smoke rise and fall within the Lethe, creating shapes that appear and dissolve, as if the Lethe were going through a catalogue of the tribes of the Green Kingdom.

Daniels looks around desperately for some kind of weapon to use. The Lethe begins to move forwards again, freezing the air as it advances and cracking the stones over which it passes.

The mist is almost upon when he hears the voice of the queen: "To my daughter, Da-ni-el!"

A bee swoops down, lifting him up, just in time. They are halfway up the wall when the bee falters; she drops back towards the fatal layer of mist.

"Too cold for my daughter," the queen's voice says inside Daniel's head. "So cold..."

Daniel remembers how he had transmitted warmth to Eireis and kept her strong and awake. He concentrates, thinking of anything hot – fire, radiators, warm milk, porridge, the feeling of being under a blanket on a winter's night – and sending the heat into his outstretched arms and hands. The heat ignites in his chest like a flame and travels through him in a bright red glow. It reaches the bee's legs with a sudden discharge of sparks. The bee is suddenly rising again. Soon they are over the wall and flying down into the garden. The bee lands exhausted at the entrance of the hive.

* * *

The hospital room was quiet except for the occasional rustling of Dan senior's paper as he turned the pages. From time to time, he looked at the impassive face of his grandson.

"Where are you, lad?" he asked softly.

He remembered another hospital room more than thirty years before when he'd sat waiting for Jeff to wake up after his operation. He hadn't thought of himself as a bad father. He cared for his son in his own way, but now he saw how wrong he'd been. You weren't a father for yourself but for your children. They had to know they had a father who loved them, cared for them and worried about them. And he'd never been able to show his son that he had cared for him, and now it seemed that Jeff had made the exact same mistake with his own son.

He sighed and looked at his watch. He'd stay another ten minutes and then take the bus home.

* * *

In the hive, Daniel is surrounded by the queen's bodyguard.

"She is there," one of them says. "With you."

Through the guard's eyes, Daniel can see the hospital room. As before, when the queen had shown him the garden, the scale is wrong. A water jug by the bed is a gigantic glistening crystal tower. The blanket on the bed is a forest of blue fibres like tufts of uncut grass. His grandfather is a giant, whose breathing disturbs the air around him and roars like a high wind.

Daniel is glad it's his grandfather and not his mother who's there. She would only panic and fuss. His grandfather will stay calm and know what to do.

"Are you ready," the guard asks.

"Yes," Daniel replies.

* * *

The queen was beneath the bedclothes. Not much of Daniel's upper body was exposed apart from his hands, neck and face. She curved her abdomen towards his neck, exposing her sting. Alone among the colony of her daughters, the queen was able sting more than once.

* * *

The composite world Daniel spins around him. One moment, he sees the inside of the hive in the garden with its vertical passages between the honeycombs crowded with insect bodies; and the hive as it appears to him as a creature from the Green Kingdom, as an endless succession of dark, vaulted passages crowded with radiant figures dressed in gold and black.

One of the queen's servants bows to him and beckons him to follow her. She wears the same long gold and black dress as the queen, but as he follows, he notices that there are other kinds of hive-dwellers: workers in shorter, more practical outfits and soldiers, with helmet and breastplate, armed with short spears. All, however, are in the same black-and-gold colour livery. And all are female, he realises. No male bees make it through the winter, he remembers his grandfather telling him. They're cast out to die when the cold weather sets in. Boy, I'm glad I'm not a boy bee, he thinks.

For the first time, he realised that it's him who's giving these shapes to the worlds he sees: the castles, towers, citadels and camps of the tribes of the Green Kingdom and now the palace of the queen. They're taken from his memory of the films and TV programmes he's watched – Harry Potter, Alice in Wonderland and Narnia, among a host of others. They reach a great cathedral-like chamber, so high that its vaulted ceiling is lost in the darkness. At the far end of the room is a canopied throne around which stand the court and royal guard, but the Queen is nowhere to be seen.

"I am with you," the voice of the queen says. "In your house of healing. Are you ready, Da-ni-el? It is time for your return to the Red Kingdom."

"I am ready," Daniel replies, though he has no idea what the queen has planned.

The royal guards step forwards and surround him. One of them draws a long, thin rapier.

"Strike now," the queen orders the guard as at the same time, in the hospital, she stabs Daniel in the neck with her stinger.

* * *

Dan senior folded his paper and put on his coat. Just at that moment a drop of rain hit the window. It was heavy, announcing a sudden downpour.

"Blast! And here's me without my umbrella," Dan senior said to himself. He sat down again, but at that moment, the bell announcing the end of visiting hours rang through the wards. There was nothing for it, he'd have to go, rain or no rain. He put on his hat and coat and walked over to the door. He turned to look down at his grandson one last time.

* * *

The guard's rapier passes through Daniel's chest and exits through his back, but he feels nothing. Then the world explodes.

Daniel's body lurches violently on the hospital bed. He opens his eyes and screams. Dan senior drops his paper and rushes back to the bed. An alarm goes off at the nurse's station. She comes running in. Daniel is in convulsions, arms and legs thrashing so that they become tangled in the bedclothes. The nurse moves Dan senior away from Daniel with a deft but firm movement and clears the immediate area of trays and sharp objects.

A junior doctor and another nurse run in.

"What's happening to him?" Dan senior asks.

The doctor does not seem to see or hear him, so intent is he on the patient. "He's going into shock! Get me 100cc of atropine," he orders the nurse.

Half an hour later, Daniel's hospital room is full of people. The consultant and registrar have joined the junior doctor and nurses. Caroline, all smiles, is fussing with Daniel's pillows, while his father and grandfather are in conference with the doctors. Daniel looks around confused, not quite sure what all the fuss is about. Memories cascade one after the other, but none of them makes sense. Eireis, the Citadel of the Argaë, the Green Kingdom, the bees and the queen – they were so real a few moments ago but now seem insubstantial as he lies in a hospital bed, surrounded by his family. But it can't have all been a dream, he says to himself. He'd like them to go away so he can think about it all, but then his mother lets out a loud shriek. She is pointing at something on the bed sheet by Daniel's neck.

"Well, that explains the shock reaction," the consultant says, picking up the dead queen bee.

"Dad!" Jeff exclaims angrily.

"I'm sorry. I can't imagine how she got here," says a puzzled Dan senior in his defence. "Queens only leave their colonies to mate and swarm."

Everyone is talking at once again.

"He could have died...."

"He wouldn't have woken up at all...."

The queen, Daniel remembers. *She gave her life to save mine.*

"If you could all go outside," the consultant says, silencing them all. "This young man needs his rest."

Daniel closes his eyes and tries to will himself back into the hive but he sees nothing of the world he's just left.

– 25 –

Homecoming

A week later and Daniel is at home in bed. He still feels weak, but he's getting stronger by the day. The doctor has told his parents he can go back to school next term, and he has a growing pile of catch-up schoolwork to do every day. Today it's maths – never his best subject. He can't concentrate on the figures and symbols on the page, and his mind begins to follow a familiar path.

He'd been unconscious for six months! He still can't quite believe it. He's missed most of the school year. He's also something of a celebrity at school. His parents have shown him the cards signed by his classmates, another one by his whole year and a third by the school staff.

If they only knew, he thinks. And then quickly adds to himself, but what do I really know? I slipped on the path, hit my head and was in a coma in a hospital bed for six months. The only thing that I know for sure is that I've been unconscious. Did I imagine it all? Was it all just an incredibly complicated dream that you have in a coma? He'd even looked coma up on the Internet but couldn't find any reports of anything like his own experience.

Ever since he's got home, he's been trying to remember everything that had happened to him. He's started a journal to write down his adventures in the Green Kingdom. His mother had found it one day the week before and read some of it. She'd asked him about it, and he'd said it was a story about a boy who visits a magical kingdom.

"Like *The Lion, the Witch and the Wardrobe*," she said brightly, but she'd given him a searching look. He'd overheard the doctors at the hospital warn her to look out for "unusual behaviour" and "personality changes" that are known to be caused by serious head injuries.

"I was just bored," he'd said.

He gets up and walks over to his desk under the bedroom window. He sits down and looks out. Now that the rear garden has been cleared, he can see right to the back wall and to the stand of trees beyond. The trees are still bare, though everywhere there are signs of returning life. He watches his grandfather work in the garden. Most days when the weather's warm enough, the old man is outdoors. He edges the lawn, weeds the flowerbeds and raised vegetable beds or works in the greenhouse, fruit cage or shed. Today, he's tending to his bees, which are just emerging from their winter inside the hive. New workers have pupated and soon will be ready for their first flights in search of pollen and nectar from the early spring flowers.

"Are you feeling better?" his mother asks as she comes in carrying a tray with a glass of milk and a plate of chocolate biscuits. She puts the tray down on the desk and sits down on his bed. It won't be long now until his little sister is born.

"Been writing again?" she asks.

"I was doing maths, mum," he replies. "But it gives me a headache."

"Never mind, love," she says. "Have your milk and biscuits."

"Mum," he begins.

"Yes, love?"

"You know when I was in the coma…. Did I ever say anything?" he asks.

His mother looks at him with that searching look again, as if she were trying to see if this was a symptom of a personality change. "Let me see now," she says. "No, I can't really remember you saying anything. Why do you ask?"

"Oh, it doesn't matter. I was just wondering that's all."

"Most of the time, it was as if you were in a really deep sleep," she says. "You weren't moving at all. Sometimes, I couldn't even see you breathing. I called in the nurse one day to check you were still breathing, and she wasn't best pleased, I can tell you. She explained you were in such a relaxed state, your breathing had slowed down, too – like a yogi." Then she remembers. "There was one time. When you had some kind of fit. It was when they tried to wake you up with a new experimental drug. You shouted something then."

"What did I say," he asks.

"Well, that was the funny thing," she replies. "It didn't sound like English... or any language I'd heard before. Almost like singing. I couldn't make out any words, and then what with the doctors running around and your father and grandfather, it's a bit hard to remember."

* * *

Deep underground the Argaë slept in their sarcophagi, safe from the dark and cold of Whiteday and from the freezing Lethe. In the centre of the cavern Eireis dreamed, a single evergreen bough held between her hands. Was she dreaming of her time with Da-ni-el? Or would she too awake from her long sleep thinking that the previous Greenday's events were nothing more than some strange illusion?

* * *

It's a fine March day, and the sun is high in a clear blue sky. Caroline has allowed Daniel to go into the garden, warning him to be careful of the path. But he notices that it's been scraped clean of any moss, and the grass around it has been cut back, so that the stones are completely exposed and quite dry. He makes his way towards the back garden where his grandfather is hard at work as usual.

"Hello, lad," Dan senior says as he catches sight of his grandson. "Feeling better?"

"Yes, thanks. What are you doing?" he asks.

"Looking for any holes or cracks," his grandfather replies as he carefully examines the sides and underside of the hive. "Wasps are terrible for getting in through any unguarded back doors," he explains. "The front is always guarded, and the bees will fight to the death if an intruder tries to come in that way, but if the wasps manage to find another way in, it confuses the colony. And if they manage to get to the queen, it's all over." He works a strip of putty over a small crack in the wood.

"Are bees intelligent, granddad?"

The old man gives him a look a long hard look. "I reckon bees are a lot more intelligent than people give them credit for," he replies thoughtfully. "Sometimes when I see them dancing, I almost think I can understand what they're saying."

"They dance to tell the other bees where the flowers are," Daniel says.

"And maybe other things," the old man says. "News about the world maybe."

* * *

A single drop of water dropped down from the surface and landed in the centre of the Pool of Life. In the Green Kingdom, the thaw had begun.

* * *

"Dan! Daniel!" It's his mother's voice. She's standing by the kitchen door, one hand on the doorframe, the other on her hip.

"What is it, mum?" Daniel asks.

"It's time," she says calmly. "I phoned dad, and he's called the ambulance. He'll meet us at the hospital. Can you pick up my overnight bag; it's on the landing."

She's changed, Daniel thinks. They've all changed: his mum, who is calmer and more in control and less worried about him; his dad, who isn't always in a rush and seems more relaxed; and his grandfather, who is more present than the times Daniel had seen him in the nursing home – they're all much happier. And I've changed, too, he realises.

– 26 –

A Newcomer

"I seem to have spent half my life in this hospital this year," Caroline says, but she's smiling. Jeff is sitting by his wife's bedside, looking down at their new baby daughter with the look of dumb surprise that is a common sight on the faces of many new fathers. Dan senior and Daniel have joined them in the small four-bed maternity ward. In the cot next to Caroline's bed is the smallest human being Daniel has ever seen. She's wrapped up in a white blanket, her eyes tightly shut.

"Do you want to hold your baby sister?" Caroline asks. She bursts out laughing when she sees the horrified look on his face. "Don't worry," she says. "She won't explode."

Jeff lifts her out of the cot. "Here sit down on the chair. Support her head with your hand," he tells him as he hands the precious bundle over.

She's so tiny and light, she reminds Daniel of Eireis the last time they'd been together, when he'd carried her down into the cavern just before calling on the Pool of Life to encase her in her Whiteday sarcophagus.

* * *

Deep underground in the Argaë cavern, the only sound is the drip-drip of the meltwater from the upper world into the Pool of Life. There are no invaders this time, and soon the Argaë will awaken and break out of their sarcophagi.

* * *

"What are you going to call her?" Dan senior asks, looking over Daniel's shoulder.

"Well, if you didn't object..." Jeff begins. He looks over to his wife who nods imperceptibly. "We thought we'd call her after mum... Iris."

The old man looks down for a second so the others cannot see that tears are welling up in his eyes. Then he looks up and smiles. "Iris," he says happily.

At that moment, Iris opens her eyes and looks straight up at Daniel.

"She has green eyes! Mum, dad, look!" he says excitedly.

"Yes, the doctor said it was extremely unusual for a baby to be born with green eyes," Caroline says proudly, as if she'd managed some outstanding genetic feat single-handed.

* * *

The midday April sun feels pleasantly warm on Daniel' skin. He's sitting in a deckchair in the garden trying to read *Harry Potter and the Chamber of*

Secrets, but somehow the adventures of Harry, Ron and Hermione don't seem that exciting anymore. In the real world, when things went wrong, like they had between his parents, or when he'd had his accident, it wasn't because of a Dark Lord's dastardly plot, or because he'd sent his army of death eaters or orcs into the world, or because a Snow Queen wanted to impose an eternal winter. Real life was never that simple, no matter how much we wanted it to be. It isn't about defeating one bad guy and everything will be alright. Real life has never been that easy.

He closes his book and looks up. There are new signs of life everywhere in the garden: shoots coming up in the flowerbeds, grass growing and tree buds bursting into pale-green leaflets. Spring has come early this year, as it had done in the past few years. Suddenly, he remembers looking out of the window of his bedroom in a dream as the garden burned, was flooded and covered in snow and ice. What was it that Hermione had said? Something about the Soul of the World telling him about someone he would meet and had to help. He tries to think what the Soul of the World might be – the soul of everything that exists: the people, animals and plants, even the oceans and rocks. But what about the machines, buildings and cars, the plastic and the pollution? Weren't they part of the world as well? He doubts it somehow. Maybe they are the opposite of the Soul of the World.

Caroline and baby Iris have been back home for a week. Daniel is no longer the centre of attraction he'd been in the weeks after his miraculous awakening. He should be jealous but he's relieved. At home, his father and grandfather are always fussing around Caroline and little Iris. He's back in school, and even there, his temporary fame has mostly been forgotten. He closes his eyes and tries to call to Eireis with his mind, but he senses nothing in return.

In the past few months, he's almost managed to convince himself that everything he'd experienced during his six-month coma must have been some kind of extended hallucination. As time passes, the less he believes that what he's experience is real. It's not as if he has any proof that it was real, he thinks. His grandfather had told him he'd been stung by a bee in his hospital bed – a queen bee, no less. But even this strange coincidence no longer convinces him that he's ever been to the Green Kingdom, or even that such a place exists. It's just another fantasy I made up, no more real than Hogwarts, Narnia or Wonderland.

A buzzing sound attracts his attention. A fat drone, one of the new-hatched males from the hive lands on the back of the deckchair. The drones have no duties but to mate with to the new queen when it's time for her coronation flight. They don't collect nectar to make honey, nor do they build and maintain the comb, nor do they care for the brood. The drone walks carefully until he is just a few inches from Daniel's neck. He half jumps, half flies onto Daniel's shoulder. Daniel isn't scared, just curious. He holds out his hand, palm facing upwards, and the drones flies down to it. He begins to dance.

"Hold on," he says to the bee. "Drones don't dance! You don't need to tell the other bees where to go." He's sure his grandfather had told him that.

But the drone ignores him and carries on: right two steps, back two steps, raise the abdomen, back two steps, side two steps, raise the head, waggle his antennae clockwise and then counterclockwise.

Daniel laughs. "I'm sorry, Mr Drone-Bee, but I don't understand what you're trying to tell me."

The drone flies off Daniel's hand but circles, staying close to his face. Then it darts off at high speed, and then flies back. It's only after it's repeated this strange behaviour several times more that Daniel finally gets the message.

You want me to follow you, Daniel realises. He stands up, and the drone immediately flies towards the back garden. Daniel follows it. Dan senior is in the house with Caroline, putting up a shelf in the new nursery, so the back garden is empty apart from the worker bees that are already hard at work collecting pollen and nectar from the early spring flowers. As he walks past them, they stop what they're doing and turn their multifaceted eyes to look at him.

There is now a second hive, ready for a new colony. Dan senior had guessed that more than one queen might be raised after the death of the old queen, and he'd set up an empty hive in preparation for the swarm that he was sure would leave the colony to seek a new home. Daniel reaches the hive just in time to see several hundred bees shoot out of the entrance like bullets fired from a gun barrel.

They're swarming! he realises. One of the young queens is leaving to set up her own colony. Daniel looks towards the house and wonders whether he should run in and fetch his grandfather. But the bees are now crawling over the top of the new hive. A queen emerges from the hive, her body still sleek and young, as she is still unmated. She spreads her wings and flies off into the clear blue sky, followed by an escort of a dozen drones. She will mate during the flight, Daniel knows, and then will lead her sisters to the new hive.

Fifteen minutes later the queen returns but instead of heading for her new home, she flies close to Daniel. Just like the drone earlier, she circles his head, waiting for him to follow her. She leads him to the garden wall and flies over.

That was where he had left Eireis just before he'd woken up! Daniel suddenly remembers, at the foot of the wall on the other side. But even in this world, the garden wall is a formidable obstacle. He can't climb it; he'll have to go around the house and down the side passage into the stand of trees on the other side. He runs back towards the house and straight into his father.

"Slow down, young man!" his father scolds him. "You don't want to have another fall, do you? Now, where are you off to?"

"Nowhere, dad," Daniel answers. "How's mum?" he asks hoping to change the subject.

"She's fine. Have you done your homework for Monday?"

"Yes, dad," Daniel lies. "Can I go to the woods, dad?"

"Alright, but don't be late for tea," he replies.

– 27 –

Old Friends, New Beginnings

The cavern was empty, and the sarcophagi in which the Argaë slept had melted back into the earth. Once the ice had fully thawed in the Pool of Life, the Argaë, led by Eireis, the first Archon and Caller of the new Citadel, had climbed to the surface to greet the new Greenday sun. There was so much to do. Parts of the palisade had been knocked down, and the wicker dome had collapsed. A team of workers had begun to build the first circular outer ring of defensive walls and dig the moat, while a second was building the lower floors of the new Citadel's first three towers. They would only be a few floors tall for the first Greenday, but by the next, they would multiply and soar into the sky like the towers of the old Citadel.

Eireis looked out across the Green Kingdom. They'd found a good site for their new home with no enemies nearby. With the great cliff at their back, their position was easily defensible. Even the Urtikai, their most persistent rivals, had yet to find this little corner, or had found it too dark and inhospitable; their closest encampments were far in the distance. But the Argaë were resourceful and hardy. They dug deep into the earth to find the resources they needed, and they thrived in even the least promising of places. There was only one construction nearby – a ruined and deserted Chadri tower – little more than a stump, worn down by the Whiteday storms.

Since awakening from her Whiteday sleep, Eireis had had little time to think about the events of the previous Greenday. Her memories were confused. "Da-ni-el," she said to herself softly. It seemed so fantastic now: an Unseen One – a creature from the Red Kingdom – in the form of an Argaë except for his blue eyes, had come to the Citadel.

The peoples of the Green Kingdom did not dream as they slept, so she had no concept of dreams or imagination. Either things were or were not. But she had dreamed once, she remembered. She had seen things that were not real but had become real. Before Da-ni-el had come, she had been told of his coming. The Unseen One had come to her with a warning from... she focused on the memory... from the Soul of the World. She knew that each of the tribes of the Green Kingdom had a shared memory that they called their "soul". She knew of the Soul of the Argaë that dwelt in the cavern deep beneath the Tower of the Lore – had dwelt in the former Tower of the Lore before its destruction. She wondered what the Soul of the World might be: the Soul of both kingdoms – Red and Green?

She remembered awaking in the cold of the Whiteday night; something no Argaë had ever done before. She remembered how the Unseen Ones had lifted her into the air and showed her such marvels! And how later, when the cold had come, Da-ni-el had saved her and brought her back into the earth. She had fainted from the terrible cold that froze her limbs and paralyzed her thoughts. Yet she had woken up in the cavern in her sarcophagus at the beginning of Greenday. She wondered if it had all been real or another vision. Had she really met Da-ni-el? Had he really rescued her?

The air above her began to shimmer, filling with shapes that she could sense even if she could not see them. They were familiar sight to the Caller. The Unseen Ones were manifesting themselves in the Green Kingdom. But why were they coming now long before the Time of Calling? The other Argaë looked up in fear and cowered until she comforted them. "Fear not. Shal-Indri have come, the Shining Ones, our friends among the Unseen Ones."

Eireis's cape billowed as if caught in a gust of wind, though the air around her was quite still. The Argaë looked on amazed as she was gently lifted up into the air on invisible wings.

* * *

Daniel races to the front door, out into the street and down the narrow path that runs along the side of the house. Surrounded by houses on three sides and by a busy road on the fourth, the tiny patch of woodland has few visitors. The residents see it as an extension of their gardens, and a few have gates in their back walls. But although it's one of the few natural areas left in the vicinity, it's rarely used. Families with young children would rather go to the local park where they can use the play areas; teenagers have better things to do, it seems, in the local shopping mall or at home playing computer games, and even many of the dog owners prefer walking their pet in the streets or park.

Daniel follows the wall around so that he is now at the spot where the young queen had flown over. She sits on the wall, attended by a dozen or so other bees, as if waiting for him. Immediately beneath her, in a patch of bare ground, more gravel, stone and fallen brick fragments than soil, three bright green shoots have emerged from the ground. The new Citadel!

The bees buzz excitedly.

Daniel's feels dizzy. He sits down and leans back against the wall, careful not to disturb the new patch of brambles. He closes his eyes.

The young queen, splendid in gold and black finery, crowned and carrying her sceptre, stands before him.

* * *

"Majesty." He bows low.

"Da-ni-el, I first saw you through my mother's eyes," the young queen says. And then adds with a tone of wonder. "Indeed, you are the bridge between the two kingdoms." She adds, "There is one here who wishes to speak with you."

A shiver runs up Daniel's spine. He turns slowly and looks into the green-on-green eyes of Eireis.

For a moment, they are quiet, both too shocked to speak. And then, they both begin at once.

"You first," he says.

"No, you," she says.

He tells her how the Unseen Ones had helped him to get home, trying to find the words that will make sense to an Argaë.

"Your tribe must be glad to have got you back," she says, not understanding what he means by father, mother, grandfather and family.

"You're building a new citadel," Daniel says.

They both fall silent again, tongue-tied in their joy at finding each other again. But then the floodgates open, and they are soon deep in conversation.

* * *

Attracted by a sign from someone whom only she can see, or whom she alone is allowed to see, the queen walks away from the pair, leaving them to their renewed friendship.

"You did well," the Soul of the World says to the queen.

The absolute ruler of one hundred thousand subject-daughters bows her head. "Is there yet time to undo the things that have been done?" she asks.

"They are but two. Do they have the strength to do what is needed?"

"They are the first but many more will follow," the Soul of the World replies.

"But I see into the hearts of others of their kind, who are so consumed by selfishness they grasp and grab at the kingdoms with no thought of their own survival," the queen says with a sigh. "How can they be overcome."

"Look at them. They don't need magic powers or weapons, because they have everything they need already within them," the Soul of the World replies. "Look into their hearts so full of joy, wonder and love. Doesn't it take your breath away?"

* * *

An unaccustomed noise disturbs Daniel and Eireis's conversation. Daniel opens his eyes and is instantly transported back to the small patch of woodland behind Greenacres. Through the trees, he sees that a van has pulled up on the lane that separates the woodland from the back gardens of the houses on the other side. Two men have erected a sign on the verge facing onto the lane.

He walks up to them. "What you up to, mister?" he says with unaccustomed boldness. I would never have approached an adult like that before, he thinks to himself as he questions them.

"You got eyes, boy," the man says, stowing away his tools, ready to put them back into the van.

"Read it for yourself." They climb into their van and drive off.

Daniel climbs over the broken-down fence and jumps across the drainage ditch that is choked with weeds, fallen leaves and branches.

His heart sinks as he reads: "Coming soon: Greenacres Wood Residential Development. Three-, four-, five-bedroom homes set in a tranquil woodland setting."

To be continued….

Appendix

Cast of Characters

The Argäe: Blackberry (*Rubus fructosus*)

The blackberry or bramble is a widespread group wild fruiting plant found all over the temperate Northern hemisphere. It produces biennial stems, known as "canes," from a perennial root system. In its first year, a new stem grows to three to six metres, arching or trailing along the ground and bearing leaves with five or seven leaflets; it does not produce any flowers. In its second year, the stem does not grow longer, but the flower buds break to produce flowering laterals, which bear smaller leaves with three or five leaflets.

First and second year shoots are usually spiny, with numerous short curved very sharp spines.

The flowers are produced in late spring and early summer. Each flower is about two to three centimetres in diameter with five white or pale-pink petals. The berries are made up of numerous drupelets ripening into black or dark purple fruits. Unmanaged mature plants form a tangle of dense arching stems, the branches rooting where they touch the ground. The blackberry is very vigorous, growing at fast rates in woods, scrub, hillsides and hedgerows, covering large areas in a relatively short time. It will tolerate poor soil and is an early colonist of wasteland and building sites.

The Urtikai: Nettles (*Urtica dioica*)

The stinging nettle is an herbaceous perennial that grows in large patches in the summer and dies down to the ground in winter. It has very distinctive yellow, roots that spread widely. The soft green leaves are carried on straight, wiry green stems. The plant produces small greenish or brownish flowers. The leaves and stems are very hairy with non-stinging hairs and also bear many stinging hairs, whose tips come off when touched, transforming the hair into a needle that will inject several chemicals: acetylcholine, histamine, or serotonin, and possibly formic acid. This mixture of chemical compounds causes a sharp sting. Nettles grow in similar conditions to the blackberry and are often found in close proximity.

The Chadri : Thistle (*Cirsium vulgare*)

The thistle is a native of Europe, Asia, North Africa and North America. It is a tall biennial plant, forming a rosette of leaves in the first year, and a flowering stem one to two and a half metres tall in the second year. The leaves are very spiny. The flower is pink purple. The seeds are five mm long, with downy bristles that help it in wind dispersal.

The Cloer: Dandelion (*Taraxacum officinale*)

Dandelions grow from a root that produces up to ten stems that are five to forty cm tall. The stems can be purplish, they are upright or lax, and produce flower heads that are held as tall or taller than the foliage. The foliage is upright growing or horizontally orientated. The flowers are yellow or orange yellow in colour. The fruits range in colour from olive-green or olive-brown to straw-coloured to greyish. The silky bristles, which form the parachutes, are white to silver-white in colour.

> The Lady Rosacea
> Hybrid Tea Rose

Garden roses are predominantly hybrid roses that are grown as decorative plants in private gardens and parks. They are one of the most popular and widely cultivated groups of flowering plants, especially in temperate climates.

The Great Kings Trees

A tree is a perennial plant with an elongated stem or trunk or trunk, usually supporting branches and leaves. Trees tend to be long-lived, some reaching several hundred or even thousand years old.

Shal-Indri "The Shining Ones":
Honeybee (*Apis mellifera*)

In temperate regions, honeybees survive the winter as a colony, and the queen begins laying egg in mid to late winter, to prepare for the spring. She is the only fertile female, and deposits all the eggs from which the other bees are produced. Except a brief mating period when she may make several flights to mate with drones, or if she leaves in later life with a swarm to establish a new colony, the queen rarely leaves the hive after the larvae have become full grown bees.

The population of a healthy hive in mid-summer is between 40,000 and 80,000 bees. Drone bees are the male bees of the colony. Drones do not forage for nectar or pollen. The primary purpose of a drone bee is to fertilize a new queen. Multiple drones will mate with any given queen in flight. In regions of temperate climate, the drones are generally expelled from the hive before winter and die of cold and starvation, since they are unable to forage or produce honey or take care of themselves.

Bees produce honey by collecting flower nectar, which is a clear liquid consisting of water with complex sugars. The collecting bees store the nectar in a second stomach and return to the hive where worker bees remove the nectar. The worker bees digest the raw nectar to break up the complex sugars into simpler ones. Raw honey is then spread out in empty honeycomb cells to dry. Once dried, the cells of the honeycomb are sealed with wax to preserve the honey.

Bore worms: Millipede (*Allajulus londenensis*)

The most common millipedes are dark brown and reach two to three centimetres when fully grown. They are round and elongated, with many small legs. They feed on organic matter such as leaves and roots. They spend almost all their time in moist areas, such as under rocks or logs and in lawn thatch.

Cloud Beasts: Pigeon (*Columba livia domestica*)

Pigeons are stout-bodied grey birds with short necks and short slender bills. The species commonly referred to as the "pigeon" is the feral Rock Pigeon, common to both rural and urban settings. Seeds and fruit are major components of their diet.

Printed in Great Britain
by Amazon